CW00536728

A NORTH
SEA TALE

CHRIS SPECK

ISBN-13: 978-1-8381273-3-6

CHAPTER ONE

In the Lord Line building at St Andrew's Dock, high up in an office behind a mahogany table, a thin man in a sharp blue suit crushes his cigarette out in his ashtray. He is balding but his hair grows curly around the sides and back. He is Henry Boyce, and because his father and grandfather owned a fleet of trawlers, so does he. His secretary opens the door, and a dark-haired man holding his blue barge cap walks in. This is skipper Richard Bird. He has done well for Henry Boyce over the eight years since he got his skipper's ticket, but his last two catches were not great. If a boat doesn't catch enough fish, it cannot make enough money.

"Richard, please sit down." Boyce does not stand as he presents the chair opposite him over the polished table. There's no need to show his employees any respect. The skipper sits, and his cool blue eyes examine Henry Boyce with a mixture of calm contempt and begrudging acceptance.

"I know what you're going to say," explains the skipper.

"Really? Enlighten me."

"You're going to tell me a skipper is only as good as his last catch." Boyce smiles. This is precisely what he was going to say. It's a line he heard his father and his grandfather use, but he won't give Skipper Bird any credit for his guess.

"I was going to tell you, quite simply, you have a final chance. I can't afford to spend my money on someone who isn't going to catch enough fish. You have one last trip aboard the Cuckoo." As far as Henry sees it, it's he who is taking the gamble. These are his trawlers that he pays for. He fits them out with nets and winches and engines. He has them painted and repaired. They are his assets that are at risk. That's why Henry Boyce can take most of the profit. The skipper and the crew just risk their lives.

"That's fine with me," answers the skipper. He takes a deep breath. "Is that all, Sir?"

Boyce cocks his head.

"You don't like me, do you, Richard?" The skipper does not want to appear rude but the man has asked him a question so he answers honestly.

"I'm not paid to like you, Sir, I'm paid to catch fish." Boyce nods at this. He was advised by his grandfather not to become friends with these rough, working people. For a man like Henry Boyce, who has been born into wealth, there is a natural order to the world with his kind at the top and the rest struggling below.

"Tadman wanted me to get rid of you right away. He says you're soft on the lads. I thought I'd give you one last chance." Adam Tadman is the fleet's runner and the man who organises the crew. It's he who gets the trawler's fitted out before they leave. He's an ex-skipper himself. Richard Bird simply nods; he is not going to say thank you. Boyce makes choices based on money and if he didn't think this man could do the job, he would have taken his skipper's ticket already. This little chat is just a way for Boyce to look down his nose.

"You know my grandmother named your trawler, I mean my trawler, that you sail. She named it after a boat she had as a child out at Dunswell. The Cuckoo."

"Very nice," says the skipper. Small talk doesn't suit him and he's no good at it. "Will that be all, Sir?" Richard Bird is not really playing the game. He should at the very least pretend to have a conversation with his supposed benefactor. Silence fills the room. The big, ornate clock in the corner ticks, and the noise from the dock outside seeps in through the sash windows with the shouting of bobbers as they unload the fish and the sound of winch cables clanging. Boyce taps his thin fingers on the polished top of the table and looks out the window to the cold February sky.

"Can I give you some advice, Richard?" he says.

"If you like, Sir."

"Learn some manners." Henry Boyce has not raised his voice but wears a sneer like a schoolteacher. The skipper forces a smile.

"I'm sorry, Sir. I spend most of my time at sea. Manners don't catch me any more fish and the lads aren't exactly angels." Henry Boyce understands what happens on a trawler in as much as they drop a net over the side and drag it along the seabed, but he doesn't really know what it's like. He doesn't know the skill, or the work, or the fear.

"Perhaps you could get a book on them. Manners, I mean. Perhaps I could get you one and dock it from your wages."

"That would be a good idea, Sir."

"Very well then, Richard." Henry Boyce has had enough of him already. He should let the skipper get back to what he does best. "I'll see you in a few weeks. I do hope I'm right about you."

"Thank you, Sir." The skipper stands and walks over the plush carpet to the office door. He puts his hand on the shiny doorknob and for a second, he wants to tell Henry Boyce it will be his last trip anyway, and he has already made a promise that he can never break. If he did, he'd lose his skipper's ticket before he left the building. It would do him no good at all. He turns, smiles and leaves.

It's Saturday. Danny's mam shouts at him from the bottom of the stairs. It's just before eight o'clock.

"Danny," she yells. She is a large woman with powerful lungs and is used to shouting. The noise rattles up the stairs of the little terraced house and into the box room where Danny is opening his eyes under two blankets. He sits up. Winter sunshine streams through the gap in the curtains.

"Danny," she bellows again. "Danny, are you up?" This is her way of telling him to get out of bed. He lays down.

"It's Saturday," he whispers as he pulls the covers back over his face. There are heavy thuds on the stairs below, footsteps bounding up two at a time. His father. Danny sits again and throws off his cover. The man must be back early from the night shift—he usually returns at ten. Danny understands why his mother was shouting now. If the man finds Danny in bed, he will be the opposite of pleased. He has a temper does Danny's dad.

The door to the box room flies open, and a big man with black hair and a moustache steps in. He was part of the Second East Yorkshire battalion and pulled out of Dunkirk in the war. He's an angry man. Danny hurriedly pulls on his jeans.

"You had better not be in bed," yells his father. "My son had better not be in bed like a bloody tramp." He saw men die when he left France in 1940 and then again when they sent him back in 1944. There's the smell of drink on him as he enters the room; perhaps he had a couple with his workmates when they came off the nightshift. Danny has been too slow. He has not even done the button up on his jeans when the man pushes him. It's a hard shove to the chest. At work, his father packs and then loads boxes of fish into trucks all night long. It has made him strong. The blow sends Danny back against the wall, and he cries out in shock and pain. His father steps forward.

"I didn't spend the night grafting for you to be laid in bed of a Saturday morning." The beer smell is heavy. The man moves forward and slaps his son on the side of the head. He's not going to punch him—he's not a monster. Even so, the leathery palm is like a block of concrete across Danny's face. The boy collapses on his bed. "You're a disgrace, Daniel. Young people today," he scoffs. "I had a job when I was your age." Danny cannot hear what his father is saying because his ear is ringing loudly from the blow. Instinctively, he covers his face with his arms.

This has happened before.

More than a few times.

The man lays into him with slaps and Danny's mother's voice is loud and worried on the landing behind.

"You'll end up killing him, Dennis," she pleads in a lighthearted tone as if what he's doing is not quite as bad as it is. He slaps the boy till he is out of breath. It's only a few more times. He is tired from the night shift and the four pints he had in The Halfway House—and the three big slugs of brandy. He steps back, breathless.

"He's a lazy bastard," says the man as he staggers. It has been a long night. He leans back against the wall and sees what he has done, watches his lad, Danny, curled up in a ball to hide his red face without a shirt. The man is suddenly angry with himself when he sees what he's done to his boy. Like the flick of a switch, the emotions change from anger to mawkish repentance. Isn't this what he fought in the war for after all, so his lad could sleep in a soft bed and have all the things that he didn't?

"I'm sorry, Danny…I don't know what comes over me sometimes. I'm sorry son." He lays his hand on the lad, but this feels even stranger than hitting him. Danny looks up through his elbows over his face. The man sits down on the bed and then weeps into his hands. Danny watches. He hates the old man. He can go from bare rage to tears at the click of his fingers, and Danny never knows where he is with him. He can never do anything right.

Danny's mam makes him some tea in a mug and sets it down on the table in the tiny kitchen. The father is asleep upstairs. He will wake in the afternoon and be as sullen and grumpy as usual, but he won't mention any of the events of the morning to his wife, or Danny. It will be almost like it never happened at all.

"He'd have hit me anyway," says Danny. His mother sits down opposite. Her eyes look weary.

"And if you hadn't been here, he would have hit me," she comments. Danny sighs and takes a sip on his tea. It's a rare moment of honesty from both of them.

"Don't slurp," she says. "It's rude." He puts his mug of tea down. "If you'd have been up then he wouldn't have done it, you know. So it's really your fault, Danny." She lights a cigarette. Her nails are bitten down and her hair is black and lank down her shoulders. She has a faraway look through the smoke. It hurts Danny's eyes. "You know what he's like," she adds. Then, it's back to the same old talk. "You need your haircut," she says, "and when are you going to stop growing?" Danny is taller than his dad but not as broad or as sturdy. He looks down at his brown tea in the mug. He wants to make himself small, so small that no one can see him.

It's ten o'clock. Danny walks all the way down Woodcock Street to Hawthorne Ave and then onto Hessle Road. He's been sent out to buy bacon and bread for when his dad wakes up in the afternoon. Danny's mam has given him a quid. It's more than enough.

There aren't many people out. It's cold but not frosty. Christmas seems like an age away and spring even further. Everyone hates February. Danny stuffs his hands in his donkey jacket and puts his head down into his collars. His arms are long and thin with slender, delicate fingers and he has dark scraggly hair that is a little long at the back. Across his top lip is a soft, bumfluff moustache.

"Now then," calls a kid from across the street. Danny's face lights up in a smile. Most people know Danny round here; he's so tall and he's a spanner. If there is something to bang your head on, he'll smack his head on it. If it's slippery on the ice, he'll fall. If the sign says wet paint, he'll get it on his jacket as he walks past. He spills things, drops cups, leaves ovens on or doors open. He doesn't listen well and worries that he'll do everything wrong, so he usually does. The kid from across the street dodges past a car and comes over. He has long hair and a tash. It's Johno, Danny knows him from school. They're friends.

"What's up with your face?" he says.

"My dad battered me." Johno doesn't know whether to believe him or not because Danny has a kind of grin.

"What for?"

"I got up late."

Johno nods. It's never happened to him. His dad is a trawlerman off Hessle Road, so are his two elder brothers. Johno probably will be as well.

"My dad's back from sea tonight and he'll have a few quid. Are you coming round? We'll get a few bottles in, me mam and dad are off out?" When the fisherman come back from their three weeks at sea, and they've had a good catch, they're loaded. The legend is that they are three-day millionaires and they'll buy everyone a drink in The Minerva, or spend fifty quid on a new suit, or buy an expensive, flashy watch. They aren't all like that.

"I dunno, mate. If I come home smelling of anything my old man'll batter me again."

"He's gonna batter you anyway," says Johno. He also does not know if he's joking when he says this. Danny sighs.

"You're probably right."

They walk to The Co-op on Hessle Road, and Danny goes inside and buys half a pound of bacon and a loaf of bread, a pint of milk, and because there is some money left over, he gets four iced finger buns from the bakery. One of these he gives to Johno, and he eats the other one. The last two, he'll save for his mam and dad.

The two lads stand on Hessle Road and eat the buns in big bites and talk through their chomps. Unlike Woodcock

Street, it's alive with shops and people. There are young mothers, stooped old women with headscarves, a hippy looking man with long hair and flares, someone in a suit with a white moustache, grubby engineers with greasy arms and painters covered in white emulsion. You get all sorts down here. Three women walk past dressed in pyjamas with curlers in their hair, even though it's daytime:

"Your brother's due to be home later on," shouts the one in the middle. She goes out with Johno's brother. It's normal for these girls to look like they have just woken up because their boyfriends and husbands are away at sea. They do not need to look pretty. When the lads do return, the women transform with fur coats and long eyelashes, like movie stars with heels and high hair.

"You'll have to put some clothes on then," says Johno.

"Cheeky bastard," she mocks, and they glide past. The two lads walk back up Hessle Road to look in the tat shops. You can find anything you want down this street from a new suit to a walking cane, a needle and thread to a washing machine or a pound of apples. When the trawlermen return they have money on their hip, and they know how to spend—what can you do with your coins when you're in the middle of the Barents Sea a hundred miles off Bear Island?

They pass Rayners on the right and it's already crammed with drinkers. Trawlers come and go all the time along the dock a few streets away. Behind the huge pub windows, there will be fishermen who came home yesterday, or those who might be getting back out to sea tomorrow. You have to squeeze as much life as you can into three days or more often than not, two and a half.

Danny and Johno stop to watch a fight develop as a group of men stumble out of the alehouse. They are well dressed in ties and white shirts. A big one with a pale blue suit drags another out by his collar and punches him round the head at the same time. Two older men behind try to pull him back, but he's too strong. They're all drunk. Danny watches as they fall into the middle of the street. Cars brake and beep their horns at the two men who stumble and battle, glorious in the winter morning in front of the pub. Lines of drinkers with pints in their hands watch the fight from the big windows and passers-by stop to observe. The one in the pale blue suit is now getting a battering, the other has got him on the floor and is sticking his well-polished shoes into him. Fisherman do dress well.

"He's had enough, Tony," shouts someone from the pub door. The winner gives his opponent one more kick, spits on him and then staggers back to the pub. Squabbles start at sea sometimes then come to a head on the shore. Like kids at school, they'll be mates again before long.

They walk past The Halfway House and on the way there, is Mrs Honeygold with a long heavy coat around her shoulders over her big frame. She's leaning on her pram, red-faced and tired from the walk. Danny and Johno both smile and say hello. There is no baby in the pram, and there hasn't been since her son last used it in 1951. The pram keeps her upright since arthritis has made it hard to walk, and, once she has drunk enough in Halfway, someone will push her home to Witty Street in it. Danny saw her one Saturday being pushed home with a line of sausages around her neck. She is a good drunk. Always friendly and with a toothy grin that shows her false front teeth. That's people round here.

At the corner, Johno turns to say goodbye.

"Are you coming to mine later, then?" he asks. Danny nods. Johno is right, he might as well do what he wants, his dad will probably hit him anyway.

Danny walks the rest of the way home on his own. He stops outside his house and looks at the net curtains in the front window; his mam says they are for privacy, but everyone knows everyone down these terraced streets. He can hear his dad in the kitchen shouting something at her. His stomach drops. Danny looks up and down the street and then back to the front door. He has nowhere else to go. This is it. There's no choice. He walks down the little alley between the terraces to their tiny back yard. Only important people get to go in through the front door. He pushes the wooden gate open and then goes into the yard and through the back way.

"You took your time," says his father as Danny walks into the kitchen. He sets the plastic bag on the counter, and his mam rummages inside.

"Did you get the smoked bacon?" she asks.

"They didn't have any, so I got the normal stuff." His mother sighs like Danny has done something much worse. She turns to the cooker and fires up the gas stove so she can start frying it.

"What are these?" she asks at the iced-fingers.

"I bought you some buns too."

"How much were they?"

"5p."

"Each?"

"For four," answers Danny. "I gave one to Johno and I ate one as well." His father cuts in from behind his paper.

"We don't have money to waste on buns, son," he scolds. Danny's mother shakes her head and does that sigh again. Every decision Danny makes is incorrect and everything manages to be his fault. The broken door handle in the bathroom because he pulls it too hard, the cat scratching on the backdoor outside because Danny did not let him in quick enough, the washing machine that does not work properly because Danny's clothes are so dirty. His existence is an error somehow. The tall lad moves to the door to go upstairs.

"Where are you going?"

"Upstairs."

"On no," says his father. "You'll sit here like a normal

person while your mother does you a sandwich." Danny sits down opposite his old man with his hands under his legs. His feet jiggle up and down.

"Sit still," says his father. Danny takes a deep breath. The wrong telling starts. "You should have a Saturday job, I did at your age," begins the man. Danny looks at the little window to the back yard. There's a small flurry of snow outside.

"I might get a job as a bobber," says Danny. Bobbers are those who unload the fish from the trawlers on the dock and so-called because they have a bob of their wages deducted everyday to pay for the scrubber – the man who washes and stacks the fish boards.

"You'd not last a day," scoffs his dad. "You'd be in tears before dinner time." Danny's father hates trawlers and trawlermen and the dock and everything about it. He was a clerk there in the sixties before getting laid off. It was a good job but now the man is reduced to working nights at the fish factory.

"I would have thought you could do something better than go on the docks, Danny," says his mam.

"They're the worst sort of people," adds his dad. "The only workers lower than them are the trawlermen themselves." Danny does not know why his father lost his job, only that it was not his fault, so he says. "Bloody animals, some of them blokes. You're not to go near them docks, you hear? No son of mine'll work there." Danny does not know if this is true. Everything he has seen of Johno and his family has been the opposite. Johno's brothers are big, warm men and his father, a first mate, is funny and friendly. Their house is full of noise and happiness with the radio or the telly on all the time. It's nothing at all like Danny's house, with the sterile ticking from the clock in the kitchen.

"You should aspire to more, Danny," says his mam. "You do well at school. You'll pass your O levels, and then you can move up. Get to university. Get out of Hull."

"Your mam's right, son. You have to do better. That's what I keep telling you, it's all about effort and grit. That's how we won the war." His face is red, and his eyes round. He still looks drunk. Danny jiggles his leg and then stops when he remembers they will tell him off for it.

His mam sets a bacon sandwich in front of him and another in front of his dad. She sits down. The man is careful with the amount of tomato sauce he applies to his sandwich, so is his wife. Danny hits the bottle a little too hard, and a big blob of ketchup covers his bacon.

His mother does that sigh.

At six-thirty, Danny arrives at Johno's. He knocks on the door but no one answers. There is music from inside, so he walks in. Mr Johno sits in his white underpants with a bottle of brown beer in one hand as he sings along to the radio. At the sight of Danny, he stands to hug the lad. Mr Johno has a big thick handlebar tash and a wide smile.

"No need to knock here, Danny," says the man.

"Was it a good catch then, Mr Johnson?"

"I'm Big Johno to you, Danny. I'm not a schoolteacher. It was a very good catch thank you very much, and I have something for you, lad" The man reaches for his wallet on the sideboard and takes out a one-pound note. "Here."

"What for?" asks Danny. He has known the Johnson's all his life.

"It's for keeping my young Johno out of trouble. You're a good lad, you Danny, I don't care what they say about you. My youngest needs good mates about him, they're hard to come by." The house is warm with an electric fire in the corner belching out heat. In the kitchen, Mrs Johno is ironing a suit. Johno himself appears from the street. He has three portions of fish and chips wrapped in newspaper and a bottle of pop.

"Are you staying for some tea, Danny?" he asks.

It is actually like heaven at Johno's house. Chips, the radio blaring, a bottle of beer for him and Johno to share and his dad telling stories from the ships that make their sides ache with laughter. When his misses has finished ironing his suit, Big Johno puts it on in the front room. She disappears upstairs to get ready and comes down a few minutes later looking wonderful in black with her hair up high. Big Johno brill creams his half quiff in front of the mirror, lights up a cig; she takes his arm, and they're off. Danny and Johno watch them walk down the street arm in arm. In love still, like people should be.

For the next few hours, Johno and Danny listen to Rolling Stones records on his dad's stereo and drink three bottles of beer that the old man has left. In Johno's presence, Danny feels like himself. He's funny and daft. They talk of many things, girls, brothers, the future, the past, school, money, and everything in between. It is 11 o'clock when Big Johno and his wife return home, and they are drunk, but not profoundly so. Big Johno shows the lads some of his moves to The Stones records. Danny has forgotten himself. He has forgotten that he is a lanky, clumsy spanner and should have been home a long time ago.

"Stay and have another drink, Danny," says Mrs Johno.

"I have to get going," says the lad. "My dad told me to be back at half nine."

"You're safe here, aren't you?" says Big Johno. "Does he know where you are?"

"Aye."

"He'll be right then."

There's a heavy bang on the front door of the terraced house. It could be neighbours worried about the noise or the police or something else. Johno's two brothers are still out at sea and are due back any day, so the smile drops from his father's face and he looks strange without it. Now Danny realises why they don't like people banging on the door. What if it's bad news? People get lost at sea all the time. Big Johno's uncle was swept overboard at Withernsea; he knew boys who went down on the Gaul not more than a year ago. If you're a friend then you just walk in. Big Johno goes to the door and opens it.

Standing there in his heavy overcoat is Danny's dad. He has a look of thunder across his face. Big Johno is instantly relieved.

"Is my boy here?" asks Danny's father.

"Aye. Come in."

"I'd rather not. Send him out, please."

"What happened to your face?" asks Big Johno referring to the man's grimace. "It's Saturday night."

"Just send my lad out, please." Danny's father has a snarl. Big Johno steps out into the street. He is shorter than Danny's dad but has a much larger presence, stronger arms, and a spirit that glows. If they fought, Big Johno would tear him to pieces.

"What's the problem?" he asks.

"There's no problem, I just want my son."

"Danny," he calls back into his house. The lanky boy appears and his eyes are downcast. He steps past Big Johno to his dad.

"Have you been drinking?"

"I had a swig."

"Did you know this was happening?" says Danny's dad to Big Johno.

"Aye. What will you do about it?"

"He's a minor. He's underage."

"It never hurt me, and it never hurt you neither. I've heard from the lads old Greenie is a pisshead, however posh he thinks he is." Danny cuts in:

"Thanks, Mr Johnson. I better get back with my dad." Danny knows that whatever goes on now will be meted out in punishment upon him when he gets home, so it's best to minimise the conversation that his father has with Big Johno.

"Isn't that why you lost your job in the offices at the docks? Too drunk to add up, that's what I heard." Big Johno feels insulted by the man. Danny's dad grabs his son by the collar of the donkey jacket he has just put on, pushes him down the street, and they are off.

They do not speak on the way home along Woodcock Street with Danny following his father's footsteps. They go down the little alley and through the yard into the kitchen. His father opens up for his son to go in first. It's here that Danny expects to be clipped around the head. In the front room is his mother with her hands clenched in worry and tears down her face. It is almost worse than getting slapped and punched—being made to feel shame. Danny listens as his father details how bad people like Johno are for him. The man explains that Mr Johnson is a known thief and a liar and the brothers are convicted, violent criminals. His old man loses himself in the joy of it and his breath smells hot, like brandy as he raises his voice in the little front room.

In bed, Danny pulls the blankets over his face as he hears music from somewhere down the street.

He can't take any more of this.

He has to get out.

CHAPTER TWO

Danny rises early, well before his mother and father. Down in the little kitchen, he eats a slice of buttered bread and looks out the window at the yard without grass and the washing line twinkling with ice. He doesn't boil the kettle; he doesn't want the noise of the whistling to wake up his parents. The lad just wants peace. He sits down and drinks a glass of milk, rubs his hands together, and puts on his boots over his green socks because his feet are cold. It's not much warmer inside than it is out. There's a cough at the doorway. He turns. It's his father.

"You sleep with your ears open in the army," says the man as if to excuse why his son is up earlier than he is. Dressed in a striped pyjama top tightly buttoned up to his neck, his father looks down his nose. Danny is confused.

"I wasn't trying to sneak around," he says. "I didn't want to wake you, that's all."

"You thought you'd got away with it last night, didn't you?"

"No. I didn't mean to be late. I just lost track of time. I'm sorry. It won't happen again, really."

"The only reason you didn't get shown last night was because of your mother," he whispers through gritted teeth. "That poor woman was worried sick. She thinks the world of you." Danny is not sure this is true.

"I didn't mean to, Dad, honest."

"When she goes out to church at ten, me and you, we'll have a good talk, man to man."

"Please, Dad," says Danny. He does not want all the attention. If there were a hole to crawl into where he could be left alone, he would crawl in it. Danny puts his face in his hands and rests his elbows on his knees.

"Do you think I enjoy it, Daniel? Do you think I enjoy explaining things to you in a way you'll understand?" The rhetorical question makes his father feel superior. By explain he means beat. His father twists things. He manages to make his action seem as if it will be the result of what Danny has done. "I'm doing it for you, Daniel. I want you to turn out right." The tall lad keeps his face in his hands and rests them on his knees. "That's the way it is, son. You've done something wrong; you have to pay for it." There's a sinking feeling in Danny's stomach like his guts are about to come out of his arse. It's the sensation that nothing he can do can fix the one big mistake that he makes all the time—being himself.

Danny stands up. He is a little taller than his father but much thinner. As he faces the man his eyes are red like he's about to cry. His father moves towards him, aggressively so. Danny steps back in anticipation. He can see the look of power and disgust in his father's eyes, so he pushes past him and into the front room. He has to get away from this.

"You'll pay for that, later," says the man after him. Then Danny is grabbing his coat from the line of hooks near the front door and turning the key in the lock. "Go on then, son," he can hear his father saying behind him, "run away. It won't make it any better. You'll pay for it later. You can't escape your responsibilities."

Danny is out the front door and pulling on his donkey jacket as he moves down Woodcock Street at speed. He glances behind him to see if his father is following, but the man is in his pyjamas and Danny knows he won't. His father wouldn't want anyone to see him outside in his jim-jams or for the gossips of Woodcock Street to believe he has anything but a good and dutiful son.

By the time Danny has got to Hessle Road, he is wearing his broad, daft smile like he always does when he's out of the house. He feels free. It's early Sunday morning. The shops and the pubs are closed, but there is evidence of the revelry from the night before. A brown bottle has been smashed across the pavement in little shards that twinkle with frost in the sunlight. The window of the bakery has been broken, and a little man in a flat cap is removing bits around the edge so he can refit another. There's a patch of spew further up outside Malone's fish shop, which is closed. Danny likes the peace.

He turns right and walks all the way up Gillett Street until he is face to face with it. The dock. Everything down Hessle Road starts here. Everything. The trawlers bring in the fish and it goes to the factories where it might be chopped up or made into fish fingers or patties, then packed and sent off around the country. Everyone depends on it somehow. Every shop relies on this business and every family is connected with it in some way. With the money they make, Hessle Roaders can buy meat, fruit and veg, washing machines, canned goods, baby rattles, beer, wedding dresses and records. Then there are the related businesses, the shipwrights, ship painters, net makers, riggers, fitters and engineers and the clerks in the offices, the girls who work in the cafés, the shops, the teachers in the schools, taxi drivers, hairdressers, the coppers who watch the docks at night and the bent lads who steal and deal in whatever. All of it and everything between starts here.

Danny marvels at the trawlers lined up together. It's hard to believe that these boats go all the way up to the Arctic Circle and back. There's the freezer ship, The Nelson, rigged up and ready to go with men running about on deck. It's one of the newer boats and can catch and freeze a large amount of fish before it has to come home. Danny watches the crew busy on the decks from the dockside but in truth, it's relatively quiet. When the boats do come in, bobbers and barrow lads fill the dock with their noise. Swingers yell from the decks, there's the squeak of cranes and the smell of the gutted fish frozen in the baskets called kits. It's not like that today. It looks like there's only The Nelson and perhaps one of the other ships leaving. There'll be a few kids there to see them off, but it's unlucky for a wife or a daughter to come. Two ten-year-olds wait beside The Nelson on the quayside in the cold. It's bad luck to carry money on board a ship so the fishermen often just throw whatever they have in their pockets at these lads. Danny and Johno have been down to get money themselves in their younger years, blokes who are still drunk stumble out of taxis and scramble their loose change. There doesn't look like being much action for the kids today though.

Danny wanders up, past the big dock cleats that trawlers are tied to. There are squawks from gulls in the grey sky above, and he can hear distant shouts from sailors. In front of him is a white trawler with rust clinging around the rivets in its hull, a trawl crane at one side and a wheelhouse with tiny square windows around it. There are men on deck and a taxi on the dock with the engine ticking over. Two blokes dressed in dark suits get out. They wear heavy coats, and their faces are red and dumb with booze. One is much larger than the other, and they struggle to get their kit bags over their shoulders from the boot, then zig-zag to the gangplank and onto the ship. Danny reads the name across the side of the bow. H.142 Cuckoo.

On deck, there's a tall man with dark hair under a dirty blue denim barge cap and a slight mutton chop beard. He is talking in earnest with a smaller man and his voice seems to flow in time with the clinking of the cables on the iron masts and the slapping of the cold February water against the side. He has gravity. He must be the skipper.

"I was told there were four more hands," he shouts. Danny examines him from far away, he has a black, roll-neck sweater up to his chin and dark jeans with big wellies. The man he is talking to has a bald head, an odd-looking eye and seems to stand with his shoulder at an angle like he's disabled in some way. The idling taxi revs up, turns around and drives off away from the dock. It leaves a space between these two men, the gangplank and Danny. The skipper walks to the edge of the ship. His eyes are a steel blue grey as he looks at the tall lad.

"Did Tadman send you?" he calls.

"No," answers Danny. The skipper looks off the docks and to the offices which are closed because it's Sunday morning. Tadman is the runner, the man who finds the hands for the Cuckoo. He must have been drunk last night, again. He looks over at this lanky lad in his donkey jacket. "Are you here for a job?"

"I dunno," says Danny. He really does not know why he is standing there. The skipper reads him. He sees his boots that are a little too big for his feet, his hair out of place and too long with a donkey jacket and sheepish eyes. Skipper Bird has very little time to sell his boat to this young man. He does not want to go without another fisherman because it is unlucky to leave with an odd number of men as well as being less profitable. Tadman had promised him four more hands this morning, and all he has so far is a Geordie with a gammy eye and a limp, who he has never heard of before, and this lad. He needs to find out some information, to see if it's worth his while talking to him.

"How old are you, son?"

"Sixteen," answers Danny. He's old enough.

"Where'd you live?"

"Woodcock Street with my man and dad." A good street. He's perfect. The skipper begins his sales patter.

"We sail for three weeks; it takes five days to get to Norway while you find your sea legs. We land as much cod, haddock and halibut as we can and then we come home. On a good catch, you'll get fifty quid. If it's not so good, you'll get twenty." The man's accent is local and straightforward Hessle Road, it has the ring of honesty about it. The skipper has appealed to the boy's pockets but realises it will take more than this to get him on board. There is no need to go into the stability of his vessel, or that the Cuckoo was built in 1964 and in eleven years has never been anything less than perfect on the rough sea, despite her appearance. He must appeal to the boy's sense of adventure and the need for companionship. What's he doing down here on a Sunday morning anyway?

"Step on board," he beckons. If the boy gets over the gangplank the skipper will have him. Danny wavers and his eyes dart over the Cuckoo. Other deckhands appear and sense what the skipper is doing. They are fisherman after all. It's what they do for twelve days in the deep seas; they pull things onto their boat—this young lad is a different kind of creature, but they will try and catch him all the same. Danny takes a few steps towards the plank:

"We're not gonna bite you, son," comes a friendly voice from behind the skipper. It's a smaller man with blonde brill-creamed hair and clever eyes. "Come and have a look. See what you think. Have you been on a trawler before?" Danny shakes his head. He steps closer and then onto the gangplank.

"You can't stay on the wood, lad, it might break," says the skipper. Danny takes another three steps, and he is aboard the Cuckoo. Four little feet clack up to him. He looks down to see a cream, wire-haired Jack Russell with a brown patch around one of his eyes. "That's Jim." The little dog wags his tail and Danny squats down to ruffle the back of his neck. "Would you look at that, Sparky?" says the skipper over his shoulder. The man with the brill creamed hair shakes his head in disbelief. The dog attacks people it doesn't know.

"He likes you," says Sparky. "Jim would have had your hand off by now if he didn't." It's the truth.

"I'll introduce you to the crew," says the skipper. "This one here with the hair, he's our radio operator Mr Sparks, or

Sparky. He's the man who listens to the weather and finds out where every other captain at sea is going and what he's doing. That there coming up out of the galley with the thick glasses, is our ship's engineer, Greasy Joe and somewhere down there below him is his apprentice we call the Rat because of his teeth. There are eleven men on this trawler, all of them have sailed with me before and they're alright. The only one I don't know is this one here." The skipper points to the man he was talking to previously, the Geordie with the slumped shoulder. The man turns and one of his eyes is goggly and looking the wrong way, all out of focus. He grins. His teeth are yellow with black along the bottom row. "He says his name is Dworkin, off Tyneside, said he was meant to be bringing his brother with him."

"Who's that?" asks Danny. Coming down the steps to the wheelhouse is a tall man with very large yellow waterproof trousers worn high on his waist and a mustard beany pulled down over his bald head. He has small, wire-framed glasses that sit on the end of his nose.

"That's the bosun." The man on the steps narrows his beady eyes. He looks like he would be better placed in a university library than a trawler. "He's in charge of the crew, and the nets and everything on the deck. He takes the wheel when I'm not there. He's an arsehole. That's why he's so good at his job." The skipper looks over at the man he's insulted. "But he's our arsehole." The bosun does not seem bothered by this. He carries on down the stairs and across the deck.

"My brother's been nicked," says Dworkin. He has a musical Geordie accent. He has interrupted the patter.

The skipper ignores him and carries on: "If you join us, lad, that'll make it twelve. The other boys are already below sleeping off the drinks from last night. Enough to sail. What do you say?" The pitch has taken less than five minutes all in all. Danny looks to the steel eyes of the skipper and his beard growing along his jawline. He looks to Sparky with his hands on his hips and his friendly eyes. Greasy Joe smiles at him as well. The skipper has provided Danny with enough time to take it all in, to smell the salty air coming off the boat with the crisp, blue sky above; and to sense the adventure biting at his chest.

"Welcome aboard," says the skipper. Danny smiles wide at this. What has he got to go back for? His mam and dad don't want him there, they've said as much, and isn't it his dad who always says he should make something out of himself? He's old enough. What is there to lose?

"Does your dad know you're here, son?" It's that Geordie Dworkin who says he was meant to bring his brother. The Skipper pokes the air with his finger.

"Of course his dad knows he's here. What kind of people do you think we are here, mate? You think I would just let a kid onto our ship as a deckie learner without his dad knowing?" Dworkin does his off-putting stare so nobody can be sure which way he's looking. The skipper runs his big hand across his chin and feels the beard in worry.

"Your dad does know you're here, doesn't he?"

"Aye," says Danny. He's not naturally good at lying, but when someone else has gone this far to help him and he only has to say one word—it's easy. He's not used to being wanted. He thinks about the beating his dad has told him he will deliver while his mam is at church. It's either that or join up, make fifty quid in three weeks, then come back to Hull and leave home for good. The skipper holds out his big, leathery hand for Danny to shake and the boy looks level into his blue-grey eyes. He has never been so sure of anything as he reaches out, takes a firm grip and feels the squeeze of the man's powerful hand.

"Welcome aboard," he says. "I'm Skipper Bird."

CHAPTER THREE

They are at a good clip out into the muddy waters of The River Humber when Danny realises what he has done. He ought to tell his mam where he is, out of duty if nothing else. He stands next to the skipper on one side and Sparky at the other with the cold grey of the Humber in front. The chunky VHF radio hisses with static and atmospherics beside the wheel and the skipper's coffee steams in his white tin cup. They have already left the gates of St Andrew's Dock. The imposing building with the words, 'Lord Line', embossed at the top disappears behind them above the wake.

"I should have told my mam," says Danny.

"Your dad will tell her," says the skipper.

"Aye," answers Danny without expression.

"You can talk to her later on," says Sparky. "I'll connect you up through Wick Radio, it costs a few bob, so you'll only have a couple of minutes."

"The things you can do with technology these days, eh lad?" says the skipper.

"My name's Danny."

"Not on this trawler," he answers. The skipper isn't rude when he says this, it's just a statement of fact. Danny doesn't understand. He looks at the banks of the Humber beside them. To the left he sees the town centre and the River Hull snaking off to Beverley. To the right is the village of Barton and the red bricks of the rope factory and the kilns of the pottery. He feels free. It's warm inside the cabin but freezing outside and the little windows are already frosting around the edges.

"On a good day," says Sparky, "trawling is the best job in the world." The skipper nods.

"When you've got the right bunch of lads, aye," he adds. "But it isn't over till we get the Cuckoo back to St Andrew's Dock and Sparky has his lips around a pint in Rayners." Both men grin and look at each other.

Danny has never been on a ship. He doesn't know what to expect. As soon as they clear Withernsea and they are into the ocean proper, the waves begin to get bigger. At the front of the boat, Danny can see banks of water, as large as the vessel itself approaching. The Cuckoo dips its nose, and they plummet down before cresting upwards on a white ridge, then falling once more. It's like being on one of those swings at Hull Fair, and Danny's belly feels like it's in a washing machine. With the smell of saltwater in his nose, and the grease from the boat, and the stench of the fish from the last haul, and the diesel from the engine, and Sparky's cig that he's just lit—Danny gags. The Skipper pats him on the shoulder,

"Right," he says. "Time to show you around. Come on." The skipper beckons and nods to Sparky to take the wheel. Danny follows through the little door of the wheelhouse. There's a lip that they step over and a metal ladder down to the deck. Wind hits Danny as soon as he is outside. It's like opening a chest freezer door and the salt spray hammers into his skin with gale force. It's hard to breathe.

"Never walk down this ladder front ways," calls the skipper. "You hold onto the bars as you climb down backwards. You have to look after yourself." When he's on the deck, the boat pitches to the left and Danny feels his legs and stomach go as his boots slip on the wet steel, the skipper looks back and points to a bar on the side of the bulkhead. Danny grabs it with one hand and steadies himself.

'Fifty Quid,' says Danny under his breath.

They go in through another door with a lip they must step over and then down some more steel ladder steps. They look through a door into the dim accommodation. It's tight, cramped and has the sweet, slightly boozy smell of men. The skipper points to rows of bunk beds bolted to the wall.

"This is where you kip," he says. "You don't have your own bunk, just take any one of them that's free." Inside the gloom, Danny can see faces from the beds looking out at him. He recognises the round, goggle-eyed face of Dworkin and there are the two men he saw getting out of a taxi at the dock, both are passed out and snoring on bunks. There are other shapes in the darkness of more deckhands. Curled up on the corner of a free bed, Jim the wiry Jack Russell has his head tucked into his body.

They walk down a little corridor as the ship banks again, and the skipper points to the bar running down the wall. Danny grips it to keep upright. There's a galley dining room with two tables at each side and fixed seating around them. Double swing doors open through to a little kitchen. Down the corridor further is another door to the skipper's quarters. Opposite that is a room for the bosun. Right at the end is a basic shower room and toilet with two sinks and a boiler buzzing away in the corner. It doesn't look clean, like a campsite toilet that has been used by many people over many years. Next to that is a hatch that leads to the engine room. At a storeroom, the skipper opens the door and goes inside. He comes back with a long, dirty white bag of heavy material about three feet long.

"This is your kit bag," he says. "It belonged to a mate of a mate who's left the business. It has everything you need in it. There'll be a toothbrush somewhere. There are three sets of dry clothes and on the top is your waterproof gear. You'll need the boots and the hat, if there aren't any gloves, I'll give you some." The trawler surges forward and Danny grabs the bar along the wall, his knuckles are white as he takes the kit bag by the top.

The Skipper faces him and looks into his eyes. "Now listen," he says. "I don't know where you've come from or where you've worked before, but I'm not gonna lie to you, this is a hard and nasty job to do. Some of the lads are hard and nasty as well. I want you to remember, when they call you a lanky bastard or when the wind is hard in your face, or when your hands swell up from gutting fish, and your feet are full of water and freezing. I want you to remember that I am on your side because without you, I cannot run this boat and I cannot catch enough fish to fill my fish room. I need you to take care of yourself and do the best you can. Nobody expects you to get it right the first time, however much they'll shout at you. Do you understand?"

Danny hasn't taken it in, but he nods with earnest. He should really start off as a galley boy in the kitchen, just to get his sea legs, but the Cuckoo is too small to need one and they are down on crew numbers. The skipper examines the lad's sea-sickened face. Some trawlermen like to treat those who are new with contempt, they want to display their obvious superiority by putting others down. This skipper has had that done to him, and it doesn't work—you just end up with arseholes. He needs a team that works together, and he'll look after this lad who has taken a chance on changing his life, at the drop of a hat, on St Andrew's Dock on a Sunday morning.

The Skipper knows more about this trawler than anyone, he knows how it feels when the engine isn't running right, he knows when to ease off against the waves, when to batten everything down and take what the sea has to give. He knows when the crew are bored or pissed off, he knows when the nets are snagged on something deep on the seabed below. He's someone you can depend on to slap your face if you're hysterical or hold onto you while the icy waves try to wash you off the deck.

That's why he's the skipper.

"Do you understand?" he repeats.

"Aye," says Danny.

"Good. Now go find yourself a bunk."

The Cuckoo sails north along the East Coast and up to Scarborough. The waves are not too rough and it's past midday. In the wheelhouse, the skipper returns to his position with Sparky next to him. He puts his newspaper back on the dashboard under the weight of a long-handled spanner, it's as good as anything else for stopping it blow away when the window or the door is open. The smaller man listens at the radio static with a single headphone pressed to his ear.

"You think that kid will be alright?" says Sparky.

"Yeah."

"How do you know?"

"It's called intuition. You can't always go on what you hear on the radio. A fella has a feeling sometimes. You mechanical men won't understand that."

"If that's what you like to tell yourself, skipper. I mean it was handy, wasn't it, that the kid turned up just as we were about to leave? If he wasn't right for the job, would you have turned him away?"

"Probably not."

"He's not even on the books. Neither him nor that Dworkin. Does the office even know about them? Does Tadman know?" Like any business, there is paperwork. Everyone on board the Cuckoo will be accounted for so their wives can collect the men's wages while they are away. Every trawlerman should be approved by the office as well, but Tadman, their runner, is probably still at home sleeping off whatever he drank last night. Maybe he fell in the river on the way back from the pub. Either way, the skipper will deal with the paperwork when he gets home. If you've got a fish room full of fish, everything is easy.

"I'll sort it," he says. The skipper looks down at one of the dials on the dashboard in front of him. He gives it a flick with one of his big fingers. The needle does not move.

"What's wrong?" asks Sparky.

"Petrol gauge—looks like we've only got half a tank."

"What?" Sparky moves over to the dashboard and gives the glass front a flick with his finger as well. Again, it does not move. The two men look at each other, worried. If they do not have enough fuel then they will not get to the fishing grounds and back, but this is not what is worrying them right now. If there is not enough fuel in the tank and the fish holds are empty then the craft will become way too light in the water. A trawler needs to be heavy enough to sink into the sea, that gives her stability. The skipper sighs. He thought he'd be able to put his feet up for a few days.

"Look after the wheel," he says as he opens the door to the steps and the freezing wind outside. The skipper goes down the ladder backwards then into the bowels of the ship. He walks past the bunk room to the end of the corridor and opens the hatch in the floor to the engine room. He climbs down the metal ladder into the smell of grease and diesel. At the bottom, playing cards on a storage box is Greasy Joe, which is not his real name, and the Rat who deserves his. The kid looks up with his goofy front teeth sticking out. Greasy Joe puts his cards down with his fat fingers and looks up at the skipper.

"What can I do for you, mate?"

He gets straight to the point. "The diesel tank is showing as half full. I need you to dip it to see how much is in there."

"You what?" says Joe. He has been in the engine room so long, over many years, that the noise has ruined his hearing. The skipper repeats.

"I said I want to check how much fuel we have."

"No need," says Joe. He has a high voice that comes from the back of his flabby throat. "She got filled right to the top yesterday. There must be something wrong with the gauge."

"You sure?"

"Aye. Rat here was aboard yesterday when the fuel barge

pulled up." Ships don't go anywhere to get their petrol, it comes to them.

"You mean you weren't on board?" asks the skipper. Joe looks flustered all of a sudden. He was not there. He met a woman of the sort that engineers like Joe meet when they are onshore with money left over.

"The Rat was here, weren't you, Rat?" The kid looks more worried than Joe, but this is not out of the ordinary. He generally has a fixed, dazzled expression. Greasy Joe tries to explain. "I was on an errand. I left Rat here." The skipper turns to the goofy lad whose eyes are round with fear.

"Did the fuel barge come yesterday?"

"Yeah, I t-t-think so." The Rat has a stutter.

"Did he fill the tank?"

"I t-t-tthink so."

"Was Tadman here?"

"I d-d-dunno." This pisses the skipper off. He knows something has gone on.

"Tell me what happened, Rat. I don't give a toss whose fault it is, and I'm not gonna blame anyone. I just need to know how much fuel there is in the tank."

"I was k-k-kipping," shivers the Rat. "I don't know if Tadman was here and I don't know if the t-t-tank got filled."

"That bastard," says the skipper to himself. Tadman hates him. He wouldn't put it past the man to conveniently forget to fill the Cuckoo up and accidentally on purpose forget to tell the extra crew that they were sailing today. He's a slippery fish. He'll have one of his mates lined up to take over from Skipper Bird if this trip goes tits up; someone who would have paid him to get him the job. That's how it works.

"You daft twat," he says to the Rat.

"I thought you said you weren't gonna blame anyone," says Joe. He has stood up but is a good foot shorter than the skipper. His fat cheeks have gone red with concern.

"You shouldn't have left him," says the skipper. "He's

just a lad, you should have made sure Tadman filled her up. You know what he's like." As he says this, the skipper understands that it is he who should have been there to oversee it himself. This is what makes him angry. He had a person he had to see yesterday. He had things to talk about that he did not want to talk about. He made a promise.

"I'm sorry, s-s-skipper," says the Rat.

"I am too," says Greasy Joe. His eyes look unnaturally big through his thick lenses.

"It's more my fault," says the skipper. "Tadman wants to do me over, not you lads." He isn't angry, just disappointed, and he knows he shouldn't be hard on these two. They're good, smart lads. The Rat will need time to make mistakes if he is going to become as good and as cheap a mechanic as Joe here. He'll need to be given room to fail.

"What we gonna do, Skipper?"

"We'll have to pull in somewhere and fuel up. I just hope to God we don't go over. If we do, it'll be bloody Tadman's fault." The skipper turns, and his boots clank up the metal stairs. If a ship this size goes on its side then it's lost. If it goes over in heavy waves, then you've lost your fisherman too. This is the North Sea not Bridlington Bay on a fine, June afternoon where you can do a spot of swimming. If a man falls in the water, he's got about two minutes before the cold gets him. He swallows. If the Cuckoo does go over, it will be his fault.

He's the skipper.

CHAPTER FOUR

"The nearest port is Middlesbrough," says the bosun, as he looks over the skipper's shoulder. Sparky taps his finger on the open mouth of the River Tees on the map.

"He's right." The skipper sighs.

"Aye. I guess it has to be then."

"There's only one thing worse than bloody Geordies," says the bosun. His face has no trace of humour about it. The words are as real for him as the sky is a dark grey. "Bloody Smoggies." The men and women who come from the port town, Middlesbrough, on the River Tees have been given the nickname because of the number of factories in their city that fill the air with black smoke.

"You hate everyone, bosun," says Sparky.

"You've never been at sea with one," he answers. "They're like leeches, they suck the happiness out of the air."

"That's what you do," answers Sparky. The skipper taps his finger on the map and nods.

"That's where we have to go, lads," he says. "I hate the Tees as much as anyone, and it will put another day on the trip, but it's either that or turn back with nothing in the fish room. We'll all be in debt to the company if that happens." Sparky wrinkles his nose. The bosun frowns. It's a horrible thing to spend three weeks at sea all around the north of Iceland and not catch enough to break even. When you get back to the office and the clerk with his cocky look tells you that you're eight quid in debt, or sixteen. It makes the skipper sick to think about it.

"It's that Geordie," says the bosun through his thin lips. The mustard-coloured beany does not reach down his bald head, and his huge forehead frowns. "They're work-shy, Geordies are, he'll cost us more in food than he'll gut."

"You'd say that about anyone," replies Sparky. "You'd say it if he was Welch or a Scouser, or if he was from East Hull."

"This is different," says the bosun. "Have you seen his limp? It takes him five minutes just to go up and down ladders. How's he going to be gutting fish on deck in a gale? He'll be washed overboard. And that eye, it's like he's looking right through you at a ghost or something."

"You sound like Boris," says Sparky. "That old git has been pumping his superstitious nonsense into your ears for that long it's coming out your mouth." The bosun gives Sparky a level and severe stare.

"I'm a man of science, Mr Sparks and I resent that comment. Just because I said someone is bad luck doesn't mean I believe in old wives' tales."

"Ladies," says the skipper to calm them. It's not even one day in, and they are already at each other. "Plot me a course to the Tees, please Mr Sparks."

"Already on it," he replies. The skipper sits back in his chair and watches the bosun put his expensive binoculars to his eyes and scan the horizon in front of him. The man's knuckles are red and bruised.

"Nice pair of eyes you got there. They look expensive." The skipper means the binoculars. The tall man sneers back at him.

"They're costly but necessary if you're to observe things in the distance."

"Do you look out your back window with them? Spy on the neighbours?" says Sparky. He is not usually crude, but the opportunity was there. The bosun seems like he might be that kind of man.

"I'm an ornithologist. That's a bird watcher to you."

"How did you do your knuckles in?" asks the skipper. The bosun opens and closes his hand to show the red bruises across them and a gash on his thumb. He pauses as he thinks.

"I was doing some DIY." It doesn't sound convincing.

"You should be more careful," says the skipper. The

bosun stares through his glasses down at the two others like he does not need to explain himself to these men.

"Looks to me like you've been fighting," says Sparky. The bosun delivers a measured response.

"I'm nothing like you and these animals in the bunkroom below, Mr Sparks. I'm only here for the money but I have enough personality not to pretend I'm friends with you all."

"You punched something," says the skipper. The knuckles are red. He's been in enough fights to know what a bruised hand looks like and the bosun has a temper. What's he like at home?

"If you must know," says the bosun, "I hit my wife. I'm sure you both do as well." He puts his expensive binoculars back to his eyes and scans the shore many miles away. He adjusts the zoom so he gets a better view. Sparky's face crinkles in disgust when he looks at the bosun's right hand holding the black binoculars. The skipper swallows. This tall man is not at all the same as the rest of the crew. The working men may be prone to outbursts of passion or anger, but they do not have anything of the measured cruelty of the bosun. The skipper points to the gash on his thumb.

"How did you do that?" he asks.

"I caught it on her teeth," answers the bosun.

There's no emotion in his voice.

Danny sits on the side of the bed and looks around at the figures in the bunkroom. They are in various states of rest, the two drunk men are still asleep and the Geordie, Dworkin, is laid out as well. An older man with a face like wrinkled fruit sits himself down next to Danny. He has a full head of pure white hair and false teeth; there's still power in him. He wouldn't be there if he couldn't work as well as anyone else.

"They call me Boris," he says. "Now then." It's a way to say hello. He holds out his hand, and Danny shakes it. The skin is rough like sandpaper.

"I'm Danny."

"Shh!" says Boris with a frown. "Not on board this boat you're not. You'll be called lad until you get a nickname. It's the worst thing in the world to call a thing by its real name at sea, son. Them's things that you just don't do, and you'll have to learn."

"Are you not called Boris then?"

"My second name's Polish, so they call me Boris because it sounds Russian. You can't give yourself a nickname either, they just wriggle to the surface like worms in the rain. One'll find you soon enough." Danny nods. His stomach has begun to get used to the rise and fall of the sea below him and the smells and the noises from the trawler.

"This is gonna be my last trip," says Boris. "The last one I'll ever do. I've promised the misses. I'm gonna get a chalet in Hornsea two-minutes-walk from the sea, you know the kind I mean, don't you lad?" Boris does not pause to hear an answer. "The wooden ones, painted white so they shine in the sun and with pansies planted out the front and two deck chairs." Boris looks off into his dreams in the corner of the dark, stinking bunk room. "You know when I started sailing?" he asks. Danny shrugs his skinny shoulders. "December 1935. I've been at sea, on and off, for forty years. I fished right through the war, saw it all, guns, mines, U-boats, the lot." Danny has heard all that from his dad. "I've done my graft though, now. It's enough for me. I remember being a young deckie learner like you, scared stiff I was. It was a lot more dangerous back then I can tell you, the waterproofs weren't as good and you didn't have no radios or telephones so you couldn't tell your mam when you were coming home. The wind were colder as well." Danny does not see the joke. The smile falls from Boris's face. "If we're to keep this boat lucky, son, then there's things you gotta do and not gotta do, understand?"

"Aye," says Danny.

"You already know not to call anything important by its name. No whistling either—it encourages the wind. Don't talk about animals, especially those that go oink. Never pass a man on the stairs. No shoes on a table. Never put a kit bag on the floor." Danny wrinkles his nose. This old man is speaking in earnest, these are not jokes. "Fishing is a dangerous business and we need all the luck we can get—you stick by me, and we'll be alright." Danny looks down at his long feet. It's a lot to take in. Too much. Boris prods him.

"You've met the skipper, Sparky and the boson. You've probably met that fat bastard Greasy Joe and the apprentice engineer, the Rat. This here is the crew, we do all the real graft. On that top bunk there, is Simo, he's a good one but sarcastic like. Dry as a bone in the hot sun." A curly-haired man looks up from his pillow and gives a grin. "Those two lads on the bottom bunks there are the Heather boys, brothers Paul and Mike. They don't say much, and all they do is work, eat, sleep, and when they're onshore, they drink. I know it's unlucky for family to sail together, but they say they hate each other so I guess it's okay." Way back in the thirties, as a little lad, Boris's mam had her tea leaves read by Mrs Moore from Liverpool Street who people said was a witch. She could see the future in the way the leaves were left in the cup. Mrs Moore said that Boris's mam would lose one of her three lads to the sea. His brothers are both in their seventies now and will never sail again. Boris hopes that she was wrong. He's been worrying about it for forty years.

They hear a banging sound like someone is hitting two pans together somewhere inside the boat. Simo swings his legs over the bunk and jumps off. He's only just a bit bigger than Danny when the lad is sitting down. He straightens his roll-necked jumper. As if by magic, the Heather brothers who have not moved since they left Hull, awake. Mike stands up first, he is the big one, six foot five or more and stocky with a fat gut. His brother Paul is smaller with a ratty face and a shaved head. One by one, the crew of the Cuckoo make their way out of the bunk room. Boris stands as well.

"Grubs up," he says. Danny and Dworkin follow Boris out the door and down the corridor to the galley. The room has seats attached to the walls and two fixed tables in front. Already at one side are the skipper, Sparky, and the bosun. They are prepared to eat with cutlery and bottles of sauce on the table. The knives and forks and spoons are not set out in a square like in Danny's house; they are dumped in wooden pots. There's a gap between the two dining tables that leads to the swing kitchen doors. Greasy Joe will be in the wheelhouse and the Rat down in the engine room. You have to have two sittings; someone has to keep an eye on the wheel and the engine.

With all the men sat down, the little room feels full, like a busy pub on a Saturday night. It's hot with their sweat and breath. From the kitchen, a red-haired man with a big smile passes out plates of steaming food which they slide along to each other. Danny takes a seat next to Dworkin, and the ugly Geordie passes him his food. It's fried fish with mountains of mash and vegetables. There's no ceremony and the men begin to eat straight away. Danny looks down the line at the big Heather brother, Mike, as he goes at the food like a dog, cramming as much as he can into his mouth before spooning in another. His hands are enormous. As they eat, Danny can hear the smack of lips and the clink of the knives and forks on the tin plates. The redhead cook passes tin mugs of tea down the lines of men. Danny takes a sip, it's sweet. The boat rocks to one side and the lad reaches out his hand to grip tight onto the table to keep him steady but nobody else even notices the swell, and they keep on at the food in front of them with slurps of their tea and belches. There's another swell, and the boat rocks the other way. A tin mug clatters to the floor and the cook bends to pick it up.

"Why don't you pull your trousers up, Vicky?" says the

bosun. "Or get a belt?" The cook turns with a grin on his face. It might be a look of shame.

"I've lost count of the number of times I have seen the crack in Vicky's arse," says the skipper. "He's one of them blokes who, no matter what he's wearing, shows his crack when he bends over."

"As long as you don't complain about the food," he says. They call him Vicky because his name is Victor and he's a cook and he's always smiling, which is what girls do— according to Boris.

It takes minutes for the lads to finish up their food and pass the dirty plates back to Vicky. Bowls now appear full of a double portion of rice pudding. The crew finish this a little slower.

"We're turning to the Tees to get some fuel," says the skipper loud enough so every man can hear. It takes a moment for this to sink in.

"How long will that add onto the trip?" It's the smaller one of the Heather boys, Paul, he has big ears and a gravel Hessle Road voice, like a chain being dragged across a road.

"A day," replies the skipper.

"Why didn't you fill her up back in Hull?" It's the big Heather brother, Mike.

"Tadman forgot to fill us up," says the skipper. "It's either that or turn back."

"It's a bastard stretch of water, the Tees, you know," shouts Boris. He has been at sea longer than any of them but has never been promoted to mate or bosun because he can't read or write very well. The word dyslexia is not one that was ever used when he was at school.

"I'll worry about that, Boris," says the skipper. "You and the lads get your strength up, ready for fishing. You just keep our luck steady." He does not sound particularly condescending. Boris does not see it like this. He's a superstitious sailor, more so than most.

"You're always making fun of me, you lot," he says. "It's not like any of you don't believe it as well."

"Which leg did you put in your trousers first this morning?" says Simo. He is the smallest crew member, and he beams under his curly hair.

"You shouldn't take the piss out of me," whines the old man. "It's not decent at my age. I've been on trawlers since before some of you were born."

"No one's taking the piss," says the bosun in his serious voice. "We need to fill up with fuel. I wouldn't have bothered mentioning it to you lads. It's not like you care." The bosun has his head tipped back so he can look down his nose at the lads around him.

"How much fuel have we got? Half a tank?" asks Boris.

"We've got plenty," says the skipper. "We just need more if we want to be out there long enough to fill the fish room."

"You know these sidewinder trawlers, if there isn't enough fuel in the petrol tank, we'll go over, you know."

"We know that Boris," says the skipper with more force. "All of us know that, so what's the point in saying?"

The trip has started badly with harsh words before the very first night. Boris eyes the goggle-eyed sailor, the Geordie, Dworkin next to him.

"It's my last trip," says the old fella. "I've come too far to slip up now. I've promised the misses I'll get home."

"You will get home," says Sparky.

The crew finish up their puddings and those that want it get a tea refill from Vicky. The air feels bad. The skipper needs to get them into a better mood.

"We've got a new deckie learner on board," he says as he nods at Danny. "Where you from lad?"

"Woodcock Street," he answers. There's broad agreement that Woodcock Street produces sound hardworking people, but that is not necessarily what they have here. The big Heather brother looks at Danny and eyes him up and down with his dumb-looking face. Simo checks Danny over also. Neither of these men seem convinced that the lad can tie his own shoelaces let alone gut a fish while hanging onto a rocking trawler in a gale.

"We'll look after you, lad," says the skipper.

"I remember my first trip," begins Boris.

"We've heard it before," says the smaller Heather brother, Paul. "You tell it every time we go to sea."

"It's a good story," protests the old man.

"Not after twenty times, it isn't." This is not an argument. It's simply the to and fro of their conversation, like the rocking of the trawler on the waves below, they are cheap comments that do not hurt.

Dworkin turns to Danny and grins with his rotten teeth, his eye is ugly like it's been scarred and it looks into the corner past him. Danny's mouth is dry.

"You be alright," says the man in his funny accent. Danny does not know what to feel, worried, comforted or both.

CHAPTER FIVE

It's dark by the time they reach the mouth of the Tees. The trawler floodlights shine on the deck and the choppy water around them. Danny stands in the wheelhouse at the skipper's request. Sparky is busy yapping into the little radio, and the bosun leans on the door smoking a cig through his thin lips. There is tension. The skipper has brought Danny onto the wheelhouse to keep him out of the bunk room where the men are a bit nervous already. They will not hurt him, but they will pass the time taking chunks out of each other verbally. Men like Boris have been doing this their whole lives and enjoy it. As a deckie learner, Danny needs to be shown how the ship works and to see it from as many angles as possible. He's good to have around. When the seamen look at the world through Danny's young eyes, they see the wonder and perhaps the terror they once felt. The lad stands straight up as thin as a bean pole with his eyes like saucers at the lights dancing across the little waves.

"There's no one to guide us in," says Sparky. This is bad news, but the skipper does not alter his expression. The sour-faced bosun does one of his sighs.

"Now, now," says the skipper, "calm down." The bosun should not be on the wheelhouse, really. As the second in command, it's his job to be there when the skipper is not but the occasion is exceptional.

"You can feel how light she is in the water, skipper. It'll be a miracle if we get through this one," says Sparky. This is true. The Cuckoo has risen in the water and is riding high on the surface as they enter the mouth of the River Tees. It was once marshland many years ago and so it is not deep, but like the Humber, some sandbanks continually shift and move. Ordinarily, Sparky would have got a pilot ship to come out and guide them into port. Sometimes the pilot will even board the ship, but that has not been possible. It's Sunday night in winter, and this trip has not been planned, so the men who really know this river will be at home with their feet up watching the telly.

The skipper knows the tide is going in. He grasps the bronze handle on the telegraph wheel and moves it to slow. A bell rings. In the engine room below, Greasy Joe gets the order. He stems the flow of diesel into the big cylinders to ease the spinning of the propeller in the water.

"We'll ride the wave in, and once we're on the river, we'll open her up." The Cuckoo bobs to the side a little. It's not something that Danny would notice, but to the three men around him, the unnatural feeling of the boat being too light sends jolts of fear like electricity up their legs.

"Call the coastguard," says the bosun. He throws his cig on the floor. "Skipper, get the coastguard on the radio. This boat is going over. Did you feel that?"

"What good would he do? He'd never get here in time." The three men know that it would take a lifeboat a while to reach them if they could be bothered on a freezing Sunday night in February.

"We're at the mouth now, skipper," says Sparky. His face has gone white, and his breathing is shallow.

"This is where the sandbanks are," adds the bosun. "If we hit one of them, we go over, and if we get caught in the swirl where the ocean meets the river, we go over as well." Danny looks down to see Sparky's foot nervously tapping on the white metal floor. The lad does not know what they know, he does not understand that if the boat tips at too much of an angle it will fall into the river. This means that the men in the bunk rooms will drown. It means that they will most likely drown also. The big sweater that the bosun wears with the roll necked collar—the heavy wool is not just to keep him warm, it will also fill up with water quickly. It will help him drown faster because once you are in the freezing waters of the North Sea, unless you are very lucky, you are already dead. Hypothermic shock sucks all the power out of your limbs, not that any of the men aboard the Cuckoo can swim anyway. The skipper sits back on his chair and takes a deep breath. His heart is beating heavy in his chest as he considers his next move. He turns to look at the bosun behind him. It does not at all look like they are in danger to Danny, but the other men know they are.

The sea around them is calm and flat as they move forward slowly, coasting in on the tidal current. The skipper has begun a light sweat.

"I think it's fifty-fifty," he says, then reaches under his heavy jumper to the inside pocket of his shirt. He undoes the button and pulls out an envelope. It's yellow with age and crumpled. He passes it to Danny behind him and the boy takes it with a quizzical look. It's something that will keep him safe.

"Put that in your jacket pocket, lad," he says.

"Why?"

"Just put it in your pocket and don't say anything else." The skipper's words are final. Danny puts the yellow paper in the inside breast of his donkey jacket.

The bosun snarls as he thumps the fat of his fist on the wall in anger. There's a dull thud.

"To go down at the mouth of the Tees," he curses.

"What bloody good is that going to do?" snaps the skipper. "You're like a child."

"It's more use than doing nothing," yells the bosun back. Sparky looks round. He must break the tension. If something terrible is coming, they need to make light of it. To admit fear is the worst thing they can do because it will not make their situation any easier to deal with.

"At least I won't have to pay off my mortgage," he says, "and I owe my old boy a hundred quid." The tall bosun curls his top lip in a half-smile. They all know the sea is a cruel thing. There's no guessing when she might swallow you up.

You can face it with your eyes wide in terror or with a grin; the result is the same whatever you do. The Cuckoo floats light on the water and outside, the flat banks next to the River Tees drift by in the darkness.

"Lad," asks the skipper. "Left, or right?"

"What?" says Danny.

"Left or right. You call it. Maybe both choices are the wrong way, but you have to call it."

"I dunno." The Cuckoo rises and falls on the water.

"Lad," says the skipper. "Tell me, left, or right? I need an answer." He has placed all his luck on this deckie learner behind him and why not? Danny will have as much chance of getting this right as any of them.

"Lad," he says again.

"Right for the fight," says Danny. It's something his grandfather used to say after the war. As soon as the boy gives his answer, the skipper turns the wheel in front of him, and the Cuckoo alters direction but lurches over to the left.

It's a sickening feeling.

The whole metal structure creaks around them as the port side and the bow are put at a pressure they are not meant to be at. It's not the rise and fall of the ocean. This is the swell from the River Tees pushing the boat back out to sea and the tide pulling them in. If they had enough weight, they would power straight through this. The nightmare is here. They begin to go over.

In the bunk room, a book slides off Simo's bed and hits the floor. The half bottle of whiskey that Paul Heather stashed in a cupboard bangs against the wood but doesn't smash. In the little kitchen, pots of spices fly from the shelf that usually keeps them solidly in place. Vicky, the ship's cook, is busy drying the cutlery he has just washed. He's thinking about if he is going to make hot-crossed buns or flapjack for pudding tomorrow.

Danny stumbles and grabs onto the back of the skipper's

stool. The bosun falls into the wall. Sparky is already on the radio, hailing the coast guard far away in the darkness across the river.

"This is the Cuckoo H.142. Request assistance. We are going over." The Cuckoo is falling, nearly to the point of no return. Once the top of the trawl winch gets past a certain degree then all is lost for sure. Ships go down all the time, it was only last year that the Gaul was lost off the Norwegian coast, but at least they'd made it to the fishing grounds.

There is shouting from inside the bunk room. The big Heather brother, Mike, is roaring with rage as he makes for the door and out onto deck while the boat pitches. He stands at an unnatural angle on the metal floor and walks to the railings and up the steps that lead to the wheelhouse. Mike senses his own doom, and he wants to land a punch on the skipper's face or whoever sent him there. The ship is pitching still, and the big man does not know if he will have time to get to the wheelhouse before they hit the water.

In the bunkroom, Boris uses what he thinks are his last words in a prayer and there is only a small mention of his wife. The woman who read his mother's tea leaves must have been right after all. The small Heather lad, Paul, who is ordinarily nastier than his brother, lays back down on his bunk—there is nothing he can do. Simo pulls on his waterproof hat and grits his teeth. Jim is asleep on Danny's bed and has his little face tucked into his messy belly. Dworkin begins shouting obscenities as loud as he can in his musical, Geordie accent.

In the engine room, Greasy Joe wipes his face with his handkerchief as he waits for orders. The huge machine makes clanging noises. The Rat sits with his head between his legs and whimpers.

In the wheelhouse, Sparky repeats into the radio. "This is the Hull Trawler the Cuckoo H.142, over. We are going over." The boat creaks and complains in the darkness, gravity forcing her onto her side as the tide pushes her stern in and the river pushes her port out. Danny feels his stomach drop.

"Right for the fight," repeats the skipper.

Another swirl hits the stern. Like a giant finger flicking the back of the trawler; it knocks the ship hard in the opposite direction. The bosun staggers away from the wall but catches the door handle to stop himself falling. Danny grips the back of the skipper's stool but harder this time.

Outside, as the trawler swings upright, Mike Heather smacks his head on a wall and staggers. He has cut his temple and is still a good thirty seconds away from the wheelhouse.

The boat rocks back upright, but they are not quite out of danger and the skipper moves the handle on the telegraph wheel and sets the speed at full ahead. Greasy Joe registers the order down below in the engine room, and the diesel engine fires up while the propeller in the water begins to gather speed. The ship levels and the Cuckoo sets off steady into the darkness of the river like nothing has happened. Sparky wipes the sweat from his temple. The skipper grins. The bosun scowls at being wrong. He was certain they were done for and wishes he hadn't lost his temper.

The skipper turns to Danny, who is still behind him.

"Right for the fight," he repeats once more. "You did well, lad."

Sparky starts on the radio.

"This is the Hull trawler the Cuckoo H.142, we no longer need assistance, over. We are not going over, over." There is no response on the static of the radio.

There is a sense of pure joy as the Cuckoo steams along the glassy black river of the Tees. The skipper visits the accommodation with a bottle, and he has a bright white smile as he enters the room, taking off his mucky blue skipper's cap.

"Get your cups out lads," he says. "It's time for a glug." The sailors all reach for their tin mugs, and he pours a good measure into each one. It's like Christmas morning. Smiles abound.

"If we can get through that fellas," says the skipper, "then there's nothing the Barents Sea can throw at us we can't deal with. I've got a powerful good feeling about this one." Simo drinks his rum in one go and then lays back on his bunk with his hands behind his head. The littler Heather brother, Paul, does his sneer. The skipper points to Mike's head where he cut it on the step outside.

"You need patching up, son," he says. "How did you do that?"

"I was on my way to smash your face in for letting the boat go over," says the big man with honest eyes. The skipper does a half-smile. Were Mike Heather to start a fight with him, he would be on the wrong side of a heavy beating, but there is a good-natured feeling to them all right now.

"Go and see Vicky, he'll sort you out," says the skipper. "It was that young lad that did it, our deckie learner, it was him that told me which way to go. He's got luck in his veins that kid has." Boris sips at his rum. He was as worried as he had ever been; now, he sees wonder as Danny steps into the bunk room and sits on a bed like he is some sort of messiah. Jim, who has now curled up on the pillow, growls without moving at the prospect of being disturbed, but Danny does not lay down. The skipper passes him the bottle of rum.

"Take a slug, lad," he says. Danny looks up as if he doesn't know what to do, and he doesn't take the bottle. The lanky boy's trousers have come up as he sat down and they show the thin, hairy bottom of his calves and the dark green socks pulled up tight above his black boots. Boris spots this in the dim light of the bunk room.

"What the hell are they?" he cries in terror. The mood switches. It's like he's seen a poisonous snake or a grenade.

Boris gestures wildly at the socks. "They're green," he yells.

"Get them socks off lad," says the skipper. "Get them off right now."

In some ways, life is already worse than being at home. At least by now, Danny would have been given a beating and would be in bed. Here, he does not know what he has done right or what he has done wrong. One minute he is the prize of the ship, the next, some sort of demon.

"Get that colour off my ship," commands the skipper again and Danny is unlacing his boots as fast as he can and then pulling off the green football socks that he put on without thinking. He strips them both off to reveal thin and boney white feet and goes to hand the socks to the skipper.

"I don't want them, kid," says the man. "Throw them overboard." Danny stands up, goes up the steps and out on the deck, into the sharp night wind. He walks a few paces, and the cold of the metal floor stings his bare feet as he flings the two socks, in a ball, into the water ten foot below him. When he returns, the sailors seem back to normal.

"What was he to know, Boris?" says Simo. "What was he to know about that colour. He's a deckie learner." Boris rubs his wrinkled chin and calculates. Green is the absolute worst colour to have on a trawler, any shade or even any mention of the word. That's why you can't sell green cars in the dealerships off Beverley Road. That's why the hardware stores on Hessle Road don't even bother buying green paint and why, should any lady in the fishing community, wear a pretty green dress on any given day, the older girls will tell her; if you wear that colour today, you'll be wearing black for a funeral later.

"That's it," says Boris. "That's the bad luck. I knew there was something wrong with this trip. I just knew it." The old man seems relieved.

"He brought the bad luck, and now he's got rid of it," says Mike Heather.

"Aye," adds Boris, as if he is some sort of scientist who has worked out the precise reason for a phenomenon and in doing so, has calmed his mind.

"Have a drink, son," says the skipper. This time, Danny takes the bottle and has a slug. He doesn't drink any, but the burning liquid hits his lips, and his eyes wince and smart. The crew in the bunk room laugh as they watch him recoil.

"I'll have my envelope back too," says the skipper. Danny reaches into the pocket of his donkey jacket and pulls out the crumpled, yellow paper then hands it to the skipper.

"It's gonna be a good trip," says Boris.

Dworkin is the only man who has not got up from his bunk, and he lays, with his face towards the wall. He has not said a word since his screaming outburst, nor did he take a drink. There's something that Danny does not like about him.

It must be ten o'clock. Danny is shattered. He lays in a bottom bunk, still in his clothes with a rough grey blanket up to his neck. The Cuckoo is silent and the river water below them is calmer than the sea. Around him, he can hear the easy sleeping sounds of the crew and in the darkness, Danny thinks about home. He wonders what his dad is doing now, if the old man is angry or upset, or if somehow, they have found out that their only son has boarded a sidewinder trawler and is on his way out to sea. Danny's fists clench up when he thinks about what might be happening there. If there is no Danny to blame then it will be his mother's fault. He closes his eyes and the guilt washes down his legs. Even when he is not there it seems he has still done something wrong. He does not need his father's indignation and accusations; he can generate these himself. Having thought this, Danny also considers the skipper and his words in the morning. He said he needed Danny and that without his two hands, he could not catch the fish he needed. This is unusual, the idea that he may be wanted is a brand-new feeling for him. Danny examines the moment when the skipper explained to the crew how he had chosen the correct direction. It makes him feel good, for no one has ever put their faith in Danny Green, not schoolteachers or parents, not even Johno, not even himself.

Before he drifts off to sleep, Danny decides it would be best if he kept his second name from the crew, after what happened with the socks. There is no need for them to know he is Danny Green.

CHAPTER SIX

At Middlesbrough the next morning, the crew don't bother getting off the ship. The skipper watches the diesel barge pull up level with the sidewinder trawler. He makes sure the bloke fills her right up to the top, and despite the other man's attempts to make small talk, the skipper has a look of steel across his face. Every second he is not at the fishing ground costs him money. The company back in Hull will be billed for this. Tadman's oversight, not the skipper's.

The skipper did ask if Dworkin wanted to come out on deck to look at his homeland, but the Geordie says he hates Smoggies even more than Makems, people from Sunderland. The skipper is like most people, he likes everyone about the same until they upset him.

By nine o'clock, they are moving back down The River Tees, with the current and going at a good pace. Perhaps they have only lost half a day, and this might not matter at all if they have a good catch. The skipper hopes that they fill the fish holds up as quickly as they can and get back to Hull. He's not any more superstitious than anyone else, but there has already been too much that has gone wrong. First, that Geordie, Dworkin who promised his brother would come with him, then running out of diesel, then those bloody green socks on the lad. That was three things alright, and bad luck runs in threes, so Boris says. The crew have a newfound respect for the deckie learner. The bosun and Sparky have both explained what happened in the wheelhouse, how if they had gone left, they would undoubtedly be at the bottom of the sea and that somehow, the skipper knew to ask the lad which way to go. It plays into the hearts and minds of the crew. They continuously look for meaning and security on a sea that could gobble them up at any second. The skipper learned that his life was at her mercy many years ago, and there's not a thing he can do to stop her if she wants him.

When they get back on the open sea, the skipper finds the deckie learner at the back of the ship chucking his guts up over the stern in the morning. He coughs, and there's nothing left in his stomach. The lanky lad has his trousers riding up his calves as he retches, and the skipper can see he still has no socks on.

"I gave you that kit bag," says the skipper as he approaches. The boy turns to him and wipes his face with the sleeve of his black donkey jacket. He's white, and his lips are pale. The Cuckoo rides high onto one of the waves and then dips back down. Danny steadies his feet. The skipper feels sorry for him. "You can change into them clothes, there's socks in there too and they're not green."

"I shouldn't have come," says Danny as he looks at the skipper. "I want to go home. I'm not cut out for the sea." This lad's voice is high and earnest.

"Too late for that now, son. We're not turning back till we've been into the Barents Sea past Bear Island and caught enough to fill up the fish room, but we'll be back on Hessle Road before you know it and I'll stand you a pint in Rayners myself, alright?" Danny's stomach rumbles. He wants to cry. This happens to most deckie learners on the first trip; they realise just how horrible it is to be on a boat in the middle of the ocean.

"My dad said I'd hate it," says Danny. "He wasn't wrong."

"We haven't even started fishing yet," says the skipper. "This is only going to get harder, much harder. You can either face up to where you are and accept it, or you can try to fight against it. There's no getting out of this now. What do you say?" This is where some deckie learners bottle it and end up in bits. It's usually the gobby or confident ones who break easiest. The ones like Danny here, who are open and a bit daft, they're often the ones you can train. The lad reminds the skipper of himself when he was first about a steam trawler, the first Lord Nelson back in fifty-nine, sixteen years ago. It seems like a lifetime. Danny looks pale.

"I just can't stop my stomach-turning," he says. "I couldn't sleep. That old bloke kept telling stories about how people drown in their bunk and how lads get swept overboard. I didn't think it would be like this."

The skipper reaches under his jumper again, to the button there. He undoes it and takes out the yellow envelope that he passes to the lad.

"What is this? Again?"

"It's a caul."

"What?

"Some babies are born with a skin membrane covering their heads and face. It looks like a little space helmet. It's rare. It's a legend among us men of the sea, if you carry a caul, you'll never drown." Danny looks at the envelope with a mixture of disgust and awe.

"That's what's in here?" he asks.

"Yeah," says the skipper, a little amazed now he is explaining it. In the world of machines and radar, of depth sounders and VHF radios, here he is, a seaman, the same as the mariners of old, explaining how to protect yourself from the gods.

"That's the caul I was born with. My mam kept it. It's just a bit of skin. Put it away, will you? It's real. Keep it on you at all times, and if you do go in the sea, you'll be safe." Danny slides it into his donkey jacket.

"Is that why you gave it to me last night, so I wouldn't drown?"

"Aye," says the skipper. He can see some of the colour returning to the lad's cheeks. "We need to be on," meaning they need to work. "Are you coming or what?" Danny nods and follows the skipper round to the side of the trawler. The best the man can do is try to take Danny's mind off it all by telling him how the ship works and then getting him to graft.

That's the best thing anyone can do at sea.

On the deck, dressed in yellow waterproofs without a hat is the small frame of Simo. Opposite him, Boris is also done up in his full waterproof gear. The yellow coats stretch down over their knees and the older man has a woolly hat on as well. He's inspecting the side of a long fishing net. There's a knife in his hand, and he is cutting extra bits of rope away. Simo has a smooth bit of wood like a big bobbin and is threading this through the eyes of the net, mending holes that he finds with a deftness that does not look possible from his raw hands.

"Deckie learner," says Boris. "Come over here, and I'll teach you how to fix nets." Danny steps over next to Boris and watches what he's doing. "I've been at this a few years," he says. "Simo here has been doing it longer than me because he fixes up his wife's stockings as well when he gets home."

"It's better than wearing them like you do, Boris." Simo is quick-witted and Danny grins. Boris looks up at the smaller seaman with false anger in his eyes.

"You'll get yourself washed overboard, you, saying things like that to a man of my age. We used to respect the old-timers when we was young."

"You've never been young, Boris," smiles Simo. It is the way the fisherman work, constantly bickering, knocking chips off each other to pass the time and keep entertained. The closer to the bone their insults get, the better.

In the wheelhouse, the skipper sits in his stool behind the wheel and inspects the flat sea ahead of him. He takes off his hat and runs his hands through the thick, black hair. It's peaceful for the moment, but there's doubt gnawing at his guts. What if they don't catch enough, what if the weather is bad, how much work is that Geordie capable of doing with his gammy leg? Will the deckie learner be okay and was he worth bringing?

The bosun steps in and closes the door behind him with a scowl across his face like he always has. He's ambitious and not someone the skipper particularly trusts. You can expect the bosun to do his best to catch fish because that's how he makes his money, but anything beyond that, he's not so sure.

"You owe me, skipper," says the bosun.

"Come again?"

"You owe me, still." The skipper does not look at the bosun standing behind him. He already knows what this is about. "You told me last time we sailed that you wouldn't be sailing again. You said you were going to give it all up and I was to be skipper."

"Well, things didn't work out like that in the end, bosun. You know how it is." A bosun gets a good wage but nothing like what a skipper can earn from a trip. If a trawlerman takes 10 quid for the journey, the skipper will get 100. They live in bigger houses on The Boulevard with large gardens and indoor toilets, not at all like the two up, two down terraces along Woodcock Street or Gillett Street where the bosun lives.

"You promised me, last time we sailed on this ship."

"I promised you I'd put in a good word with the office, that's all. I said that if things went well with the trip, I'd be leaving and that you'd be the next in line. The catch was crap, you know that." He doesn't have to be truthful with this man. "Things didn't go well ashore, mate. It didn't go as I wanted it to, and so, for the foreseeable, I'm here. Alright?" The last word is not meant as a question, although it's framed as one. It's meant to be a statement that is stuffed down your throat whether you like it or not.

"Do you know how many years I've worked ships?"

"No, but I've got a feeling you're about to tell me."

"Twenty-five years, and you got made a skipper before me. It turns my stomach, it does. You're too young. I told them, too young for the job. Not enough experience. Not tough enough by a long way." The bosun hates everyone and everything, but he has a special kind of seething anger for this skipper whose job he thinks he should have. "You just fritter away your money like these other bloody fools, think what a man like me could do with a wage like that." The bosun has a thin, reedy wife back on Gillett street. She lives with his elderly mother, but it is her wish after she has scrimped and saved for so many years, for them to get out of the noise and stink of Hessle Road to the West Hull Villages like Kirkella or Willerby. Like she has told her husband, she won't be happy until she gets on up and he makes something of himself. She gives as good as she gets.

Now, the skipper turns to his bosun. "They made me skipper, bosun, because the men don't like you. They can't work with someone they don't trust, so rather than getting at me, why not look at what's wrong with you?"

"If we weren't on board this ship, I'd slap you back to the gutter you crawled out of," sneers the bosun. The skipper stands. He's a few inches smaller but broader.

"You watch the way you speak to me, bosun. I'm still the skipper. If it comes to it, I can put you on your arse."

"You wouldn't dare."

"Try it." The bosun takes a breath in through his nose and sneers. He thinks about his wife back in Gillett street, the tears rolling down her face when he told her he had not been sent to get his skipper's ticket. He needs that job.

"It would be horrible if something happened to you, skipper," says the bosun.

"I'll pretend I didn't hear that," he whispers. "It's more likely something will happen to you, the way you speak to people. Don't think I don't know what you're up to as well, with that camera."

"What do you mean?"

"It's obvious, isn't it?"

"I take pictures, what's obvious about that?" The bosun has an expensive long lens camera in a waterproof case in his cabin as well as those binoculars. In his desk draws there are ring bound pamphlets with silhouettes of Russian warships and submarines.

"I wouldn't like to let the lads know what you are up to, especially after what happened to the Gaul." The bosun's face flushes a deep red. He prods the skipper in his chest with a slender finger.

"That's my hobby," he whispers. "I think it would be best all round if it wasn't mentioned." It's still the cold war, and Hull trawlers are tolerated vessels in the northern waters of the Barents Sea and even the White Sea off the coast of Russia. There's a rumour that the Gaul was sunk by a USSR submarine because it was spying—just a rumour, but trawlermen do get paid to photograph what they've seen, especially someone as shifty as the bosun. Some man in a suit with a big wallet will have told him to note down everything he sees out on the ocean and if he can, photograph it. Now the skipper has seen the way the bosun reacts to the accusation, he knows he's working for someone.

"It's not fair on the crew," says the skipper. "If we get boarded by a foreign navy, and they ask who the spy is, I'll tell them it's you to protect these lads, straight away." The bosun's hands clench into fists. It's not unusual for The Russians to keep an eye on a trawler that gets too close, nor for them to board a ship even. It's their waters, it's their right.

"You wouldn't understand the reasons, skipper. A man like you doesn't understand his duty."

"To those grey suits? Not only do we risk our lives to put fish on their plates, but we do their bloody espionage for them too?" The skipper shakes his head. "They're taking the piss out of you, bosun, just like everyone else."

Sparky enters and claps his hands together from the cold

after he closes the door. He sees the look of anger on the two men's faces.

"Don't mind me, ladies," he says as he brushes past the skipper. He knows there's bad blood between these two, but now that he's there, they will not say another word. The integrity of the ship is their life as well as their money and any squabbles they have will be kept away from the other men. Sparky sits himself down in front of the radio and sticks the headphones on. The air bristles between the two men.

"I've heard something on the wireless already," says Sparky. "The skipper from the Arctic Hunter on to the office back in dock."

"When?" asks the skipper.

"This morning, I didn't want to say anything too soon or get you too excited."

"Spit it out," says the bosun.

"The radio operator says he's getting dressed up for a good night out." The bosun wrinkles his nose, and the skipper smiles.

"What was the answer?"

"The office told him to stay out as long as he needs to." The seabed of the Barents fishing grounds is every bit as rugged and varied as the forest or the mountains on land. Where they drag the nets there are gullies and canyons, peaks and troughs, places to get your trawl snagged, parts where some skippers are lucky, and others are not. Since the twenties, skippers, bosuns and mates have scribbled in their notebooks and drawn maps so that these underwater cliffs and hills have names like the constellations in the sky. There's The Baby's Foot, Hari Kari Bank, Kidney Bank and a hundred more.

"It's The Top Hat," says the skipper. "Getting dressed up, that's where the Arctic Hunter is then, Sparky. She's at the Top Hat." The man with the brill-creamed hair smiles back at him. The Top Hat is one of these underground banks, shaped like the posh headgear worn by toffs of antiquity.

"Then that's where we'll go," says the bosun. "We'll bag two hundred and twenty tonne, and then we're home."

Between them, Boris and Simo explain how a sidewinder trawler goes about its fishing; they go into a depth of description that is hard to follow for Danny. Each man tries to outdo the other in terms of specific knowledge and seafaring wisdom. Simo explains how they drop the net into the water by hand and with the trawl winch. Then Boris goes into the fine detail of how many holes there should be in each part of the net. Next, Simo tells Danny about the trawl winch and then the fish washer and how, after you've gutted the fish, it goes down into the fish room where it is stored on aluminium trays with ice and separated by boards. Simo explains the process of packing. Danny feels his brain sagging with too much information as big Mike Heather walks up beside them and looks down on the men talking. He has a reputation for being a bit of an idiot, perhaps because of his size but Mike has a gift for seeing simplicity where others see complication.

"You pull the net out of the sea, drop the fish on deck, cut out their guts and throw them into that machine. When we get to the Barents Sea, that's what you do for eighteen hours a day." The honesty forces the other men to quieten down. "You've filled his head with enough shite already," says Mike. Simo does not come back with anything sarcastic to this big man, and Danny senses that he does not take well to being made fun of. They fall back to mending the nets.

Mike opens a big toolbox and tuts when he sees what a mess it's in. Danny stands next to him. It's everyone's job to train a deckie learner, just like it's everyone's job to do everything on a ship. Mike begins to take tools out of the box and unwraps them from the greasy rags. If the crew can teach this lad how to do his job then he will help them land more fish and therefore they will make more money. Mike begins to explain.

"You need three of everything," he says as he counts out three of the crocodile jawed spanners. "Not just these tools, you need three pairs of socks, three pairs of trousers, three gutting knives, three hats because you're going to get wet and things are going to get broken. If the boat hits a good patch of fish you can pull up fifty tonne in twenty-four hours. We've gotta be ready. These tools need to be ready."

There's the sound of footsteps behind. It's the bosun. When Mike Heather sees who it is, he goes back to the job he's working on. The tall man with the mustard beanie sees Jim sat on his hind legs, he boots the little dog with a flick of his foot. The creature yelps and scuttles off with its tail between its legs. Mike looks at him in disgust. There was no need for that and it's a good job the skipper didn't see him do it.

"Dogs shouldn't be on ships," he says. "Showing our Deckie Learner the ropes are you, Heather?" The big man just grunts in response to someone he does not have any respect for. The bosun is not here to speak to him, he's for the boy.

"Deckie learner," says the bosun and Danny nods. "As this is your first time on the ship, when we do get to dragging the nets on board and gutting, I want you in the wheelhouse. The last thing we need is you washed overboard. It would cost us a fortune." Mike Heather stands up and looks quizzical at the bosun.

"We're two men down, we need every hand on the deck and gutting too, if it's busy."

"I wasn't asking you."

"We'll need him with a knife in his hand if we start hauling in big," yells Simo.

"I was straight on the decks on my first trip out," said Boris, "and that was back when it was a real man's job."

"And me," adds Simo. They are playing with the bosun. If he had come down and told young Danny that he had to stand and gut with the rest of the crew when the fish start coming in, they would have told him it was too dangerous for a lad. They would have said they spent their first trip getting their sea legs with the skipper and learning the ropes while sipping tea in the wheelhouse. The bosun looks down at his feet and does a dramatic sigh. It doesn't matter what he thinks, the skipper will decide anyway.

"Make sure you find all the holes, lads," says the bosun as he steps away. "And make sure there's three of everything in there," he calls to Heather. The big man grunts. Another has joined them on deck. It is the wiry frame of the smaller Heather brother, Paul. He has a thin moustache with a twisted nose from having it broken more than once and in different ways.

"Nice hat there, bosun," he remarks. "Did your misses wash it the day we sailed?" The thin bosun flares his nostrils. Paul Heather has little to no charm about him.

"She would never do that," says the bosun. He doesn't want to get drawn into a fight that he would have to win.

"I heard she washes all your clothes the day you leave," says Paul Heather, "and, that she has done for years. Then every time she sees you sailing back into the dock home, she weeps into her hands."

"Out of my way," says the bosun. His face is creased with anger. Many people have heard this story. The bosun has heard it too. If a wife washes her husband's or son's clothes the day he sails, she washes away all his luck and washes him out to sea with it. Not a soul on Hessle Road would do this but, Paul Heather's mam knows a girl on Gillett street who is friendly with the bosun's thin and aloof wife. There have been whispers that she forced her husband to take out an expensive life insurance policy in case anything happened to him out at sea, and that also, she washes his socks and his mustard-coloured beanie the day he leaves. It's something to have a laugh about. The bosun is not smiling as he looks in the sea-green eyes of Paul Heather on the deck of the Cuckoo three days away from Bear Island.

Sparky appears:

"Every time I see you, bosun, you're about to start a fight." He has a friendly voice as he leans on the bars of the steps leading down from the wheelhouse. The bosun snarls at him and then brushes past Paul Heather. When he is sure the man is out of earshot, Mike Heather calls out loudly to his brother.

"You shouldn't take the piss out of him. Like the skipper says, he's an arsehole, but he's our arsehole."

"He's just an arsehole," says Paul Heather.

CHAPTER SEVEN

The skipper has sent Danny to the engine room to look around and find out what drives the ship. The tall lad has felt less seasick since he has had something to worry about and the trawlermen have all told him to enjoy the next few days because, when they get to the Barents Sea, things will become unpleasant. He has also heard that they are bound for The Top Hat, and the weather will not be good. Danny does not know what to expect, but when big men like Mike Heather tell him to prepare for the worst and even the skipper shakes his head and sucks in breath, he knows it will be bad. The crew will make it sound more awful than it will be for Danny. It's a kindness. When the lad does start gutting on the open deck, he will find out that it is cold, hard and dreary. He will not be afraid after an hour because he will be in too much pain. He opens the big hatch then clanks down the steps.

At the bottom a few feet away, is an enormous engine, painted bright yellow. Pipes feed it from all angles. Some are painted brown and others blue. It looks like some oversized child's toy. Out of the sharp wind, Danny's ears begin to burn. The noise of the gale is replaced by the clanking from the heart of the trawler and the stink of fish guts replaced by diesel and grease. Joe appears, he is wearing dungarees over a dirty blue t-shirt. He is fatter than the rest of the crew, and he looks up at Danny with squinting eyes through his thick, black glasses.

"What do you want?" he asks.

"The skipper sent me to learn about the engine." Joe nods. He is happy to oblige. The Rat appears wearing the same kind of dirty dungarees under a jacket with black hair and his buck teeth sticking out. The Rat is not scared of Danny because, in the hierarchy of the boat, the deckie learner is lower even than himself. Danny follows these two engineers in the heat and the noise. Greasy Joe calls out to him in explanation.

"It's a 1000 horsepower engine, that's the bit in yellow. The brown pipes carry oil, and the blue ones carry freshwater. The black one is bile. That's the pump there. It doesn't stop till we get back to Hull." He might as well be showing Danny the inner workings of a spaceship or someone's stomach for the words and ideas go clear over his head. Joe, however, is clearly passionate about his domain. He points to a row of pistons that power the propellers at the back of the ship, sunk into the freezing water of the North Sea.

"That's what drives us and I'm the only one who knows how it works, that's why I'm the most important person on this boat," shouts Joe with a grin. "They'll all tell you how hard and dangerous it is gutting fish, but without this engine here, the Cuckoo might as well be a lump of rust. The second most important person is the Rat here." The boy next to him, nods and grins. Greasy Joe wipes sweat from his forehead with a handkerchief. Up on deck, he is a slightly fat, shy man with thick window glasses, Danny can see that he is something much more down here. He passes Danny a rag and bids him to follow as he and the Rat move to one of the massive piston heads that is not moving. The Rat leans over and begins to rub off thick dirt and grime, Joe does the same, and then Danny leans in to help also. He does not notice the pitch and fall of the boat as he works, and he builds up a light sweat. He watches Joe stand up and inspect a row of dials, wipe his hand off and make a note in an official-looking book. If Danny or his father were to walk past Joe or the Rat on Hessle Road, looking as they do, he might think they were daft lads or thickos, those that cleaned factory floors or machines. Now he sees something different in Rat's shrewd eyes as he examines one of the moving piston heads. Like all the men aboard the Cuckoo, those onshore underestimate their skill and intelligence. Men like Danny's father do not credit their worth. Out here in the sea, hundreds of miles from anywhere, they might as well be on the surface of the pale moon.

"They all think I'm stupid, up there," shouts Joe. Danny nods. "That Paul Heather and his brother. They're bloody animals if you ask me. The skipper's alright though, he's one of us, isn't he, Rat?" The boy nods. "But that bloody bosun, he looks down his nose at the Rat and me here. You know his misses washes his clothes on the day he sails," grins Joe. Danny nods and smiles. "I heard he wants his skipper's ticket. He just needs the company to give him the job. I'd never sail with him as skipper, would you Rat? I'd sooner sail under Boris."

"Does it ever break down?" asks Danny. He does not actually want to know the answer, but he has found people like to talk, and if he can keep them talking then they will be happier. Danny likes it when people are happy.

"You better hope she doesn't, lad," says Joe. The fat man is polite and glad that someone sees and respects what he does. In fact, if Danny and his father were to walk past Greasy Joe and the Rat on Hessle Road, it would be these two skilled engineers who would look with disdain on them rather than the other way round. Joe glances at his watch and then back to the Rat.

"It's dinner time," he shouts, though there is no need to be so loud. "You go first, Rat," says Joe. There always has to be someone with the engine. The young man nods. Danny follows him up the steps and through the hatch. When they get up to the corridor outside the bunk room and it's just the two of them, the Rat turns:

"You better not g-g-give me any trouble," he snarls, "or I'll s-s-smash your face in." It is unprovoked, and Danny frowns at this. He does not know what he has done as he steps back. For the Rat, however, it makes perfect sense.

Onboard the Cuckoo, this deckie learner is lower than he is, so he can treat him badly in just the same way as the older crew treat the Rat. It's not quite how it really works, but in the apprentice engineer's mind, he is spot on.

"You just d-d-do as I tell you." It's sometimes the most bullied that are the bullies themselves. Danny wrinkles his nose at this lad with his buck teeth and thin neck. He doesn't know how to respond to this threat and Danny isn't an aggressive lad, so he shrugs it off.

"Alright," he says.

"G-G-Good," answers the Rat.

It's the first sitting of dinner. The Skipper and Sparky are in the wheelhouse. More than half the crew sit down in the little galley at the dining tables, and Vicky passes them plates of food which they slide down on either side. There's a yelp from little Jim as the bosun kicks him out from under the table with unreasonable force.

"We should put that dog overboard for Christ's sake," he shouts. "They've got no place on a bloody boat, let alone a galley where we eat." There are nasty glances but this tall man is ignored. Each plate is loaded again with two lightly fried pieces of cod and a big pile of chips and some beans.

"I hope you like fish," says Dworkin who is sitting next to Danny. "That's all they serve on these boats." The Geordie sounds as if he doesn't like it, but he tucks into his quickly enough. Danny has not seen this strange-looking man do any work yet, and he does not engage in the style of banter that the others do. Every so often he sighs and sometimes sneers to himself when they crack off a good one, or when Mike Heather delivers one of his large, overly wet farts without expression. The crew comments on Vicky's cooking as they eat.

"I'm not having this for three weeks," says Simo with his sarcastic, dry tone. Nobody answers this. The trawlermen will eat fish for three weeks for lunch, and for supper if there's any left from the day, and for breakfast if they want. "I thought you were going off to college to learn how to be a proper cook, Vicky, that's what you said on the last trip." Vicky looks at Simo under his ginger hair with a slight frown and a nervous grin. "Can you speak French?" he asks. It's best not for Vicky to answer, he's too gentle to get involved with the tit for tat and almost always comes off with everyone laughing at him. He passes out tea in tin mugs. Danny takes a sip.

"What boats have you been on?" Danny asks Dworkin. The man looks across at him, his right eye is disfigured and unnerving to look at with the pupil staring at the corner of the room.

"Tonnes," he answers in his Geordie accent, "I started on The Jeannie Steward in 1967 out of Tyneside and The Newson in 1970, both sidewinders like this, both a bit bigger with a few more hands." He says it loud enough so that everyone can hear.

"The Steward went down, I heard," says the bosun.

"Aye, it did. I was meant to be on it, too." There are no cheap jokes about this. "I was at home the night before, and there was a bang from downstairs in the front room. When I went down and turned on the light, the mirror from above the fireplace had fallen off the wall and smashed." Boris raises his eyebrows at this and Paul Heather stops eating to look at the Geordie mariner. "After that, I didn't bother going to the dock the next morning. The skipper sent the bosun to get us, and I told him that me and my brother weren't getting on board, not after that mirror fell. It was a sign."

"Aye," says Boris. "The Steward was lost then?"

"All hands."

The crew are silent.

"Is that where you injured your eye?" It's Simo, his tone

again sarcastic. None of the men want to dwell on this story that proves the superstitions they hold are true and valid. They would rather take the piss, to lighten the mood.

"I was born like this," answers Dworkin.

"Handsome lad, aren't you?" This time, it's Paul Heather. Dworkin does not answer. The man's voice has an unpleasant tone, but the Geordie has heard every insult that can be imagined about his eye. It does not bother him anymore.

"I heard you snoring last night, Boris," says Simo as he puts his mug of tea down. He has a cheeky grin. "Like a baby, you were, on your front." He is winding the old man up. Fishermen know you should never sleep on your stomach, it's symbolic of the boat capsizing.

"Always bloody joking aren't you, Simo? I was on my back last night like I always am. You shouldn't make fun of these things, it's bad luck."

From near the kitchen, the bosun pipes up:

"What a load of shite," he calls. "You poor bastards are living in the dark ages." The bosun pretends he is the voice of reason. When he was younger, because of his brains, he won a scholarship to a posh school on Spring Bank West. It's a leafy old-style grammar that gives out a few free places to intelligent, poor kids to show that it cares about the city. The bosun's father was mistrustful of its grandeur and did not let his son go. It was not a big blow, but it did fix in the bosun's mind that he is significantly more intelligent than everyone else around him.

"You better watch your mouth," snaps Boris back. "Be bloody careful what you say, for your own sake."

"I've been at sea for twenty-five years," he says. "Twenty-five years and nothing has happened to me. I've talked about pigs on a ship, and I've got loose change in my wallet right now. I've worn green underpants, I whistle when I'm on the toilet." He bangs the flat of his hand on the table, and it rattles his plate. "Like you bastards tell me, my wife washes my clothes on the day I sail, and I'm still standing here. I broke a shaving mirror before I left my house yesterday morning. I forgot my toothbrush, so I just turned round and went back for it." It's an unnecessary rant. The man has broken many taboos. No one is smiling. The only sound is Mike Heather as he chomps down his piece of lightly fried fish and his lips smack.

"You'll bring bad luck on yourself, bosun," says Paul Heather.

"I make my own luck," replies the bosun. "It would be best if you did the same, you might make something of yourselves." The bosun stands, and his face is one of disgust. Even Danny can see that this angry man should never be a skipper by the way he talks to people. He shouldn't be a bosun. He makes his way out of the room and the crew watch him go with flat, expressionless eyes.

Afters is bread and butter pudding with raisins and custard. It's not too bad. The crew make their way out, and the skipper and Sparky enter now they've been relieved. Greasy Joe joins them. On a bigger ship, there would be two galleys, one for the more senior crew and the other for the lowly deckhands. On the Cuckoo, they all have to eat together and the chief engineer, Greasy Joe, doesn't even get his own room. The skipper directs Danny to the cook and the little galley kitchen through the swing door.

"Help our Vicky wash the pots, will you, lad?" It's not a question, and Danny finds himself walking through the double doors to where Vicky is smiling back at him. The big red-headed man wears a chef's top and checkered trousers.

"Now then," he says. "Grab a cloth and dry these." The cook has his hands in water, and scrubs plates without looking then puts them on the rack beside the sink in a holder. Danny grabs one and nearly drops it because the water is so hot. Vicky has a kind of dumb grin stuck to his face and his greasy ginger hair is combed to the side.

"How are you finding it?" he asks. Danny does not have time to answer before Vicky replies. "Shite, innit? But the money is good if we get a good catch." The lanky boy dries the plates and sets them back in the drawers where Vicky shows him. The red-head babbles on. "We've got the best skipper on the docks, you know. Dickie Bird. I've sailed with him for years, through storm and gale, eight years now. This is the best trawler for its size in Hull." Vicky's head and gob seem to be independent of his body and he goes on explaining the good things of the world around them. "The fish is good, fresh like it's just come out of the ocean, that bread and butter pudding was a good job as well." There's a pause while he clanks around with some plates. "That Simo makes me laugh though, doesn't he you?" and then, "When I first started on the Cuckoo, there wasn't a shower room. It was just a bucket. It's the skipper that's got it for us," says Vicky. "He's the best skipper on Hessle Road, maybe in the whole of Hull, maybe even on the North Sea. Dickie Bird. They say he can drink twenty pints in a night as well. Paul Heather's a hard bastard and so is his brother, and anything you want to know about fishing, you can just ask Boris. He's been everywhere." Danny gets the feeling that Vicky could go on without him being there.

"Where are you from then, son?" asks the cook.

"Woodcock Street."

"Do you know Kevin Spencer?" Everyone knows everyone else down Hessle Road, somehow.

"I know Catherine Spenser, aye."

"Well, you won't know her dad. A few summers ago, he painted the fence outside his house bottle green, I heard. He was five days into his trip on the Joseph Conrad Trawler when a wave washed him off into the sea. They said he was there one minute and not the next." The cook pauses for effect. "So, you see, our Boris isn't soft." Danny continues to dry plates. "They're all good ones on here, all of them. I don't know that Dworkin fella yet, but he looks steady on his feet, even though one of them is lame." Vicky stops scrubbing at a big pan for a moment and turns to the boy. "Be careful of that bosun though, lad. He's a right one. This might be his last trip so I've heard. I know that the skipper doesn't like him and if he doesn't like someone, then neither do I." Once he has washed all the pots, he goes to work on the cooker with a cloth and scrubs off the muck. He continues to detail the best things about the world, and it's good for Danny to listen to. He explains the best barmaids on Hessle Road and the best pubs, the best Led Zeppelin record, the best way to win at cribbage, the best horses to bet on and many times, the best skipper he has ever known. Richard 'Dickie' Bird.

Vicky half fills a big kettle with water and boils it on the gas stove. He has explained where to put all the plates, the pots, the cutlery and the tin mugs. Everything has its place in the galley kitchen. There's a clang and a noise from inside the boat and suddenly, music sounds, tinny and far away.

"Thank God for that," says Vicky. "Sparky must have fixed the wireless." Radio Luxembourg flows through the bunk room and the skipper's quarters into the galley and onto the deck. It's The Joker by the Steve Miller Band, cool and American. About as far away from the North Sea as you can get.

The first set of crew sit down to have their evening tea, they dip biscuits in the dark brown liquid from a teapot that Vicky has explained must never be emptied. Danny feels at home, somehow, though he has only been on board a few days. Boris, the Heather brothers and Simo swap stories of the sea and Danny listens in.

"I was meant to be on St. Romanus," says Simo. "My girlfriend at the time was in hospital having her tonsils out, and she didn't want me to go away so I stayed. The best decision I ever made." The St. Romanus went down with all hands in 1968. The first of three trawler tragedies that same year. "I married her after that," said Simo. "I thought she was lucky." Boris nods at this.

"It was better before the war," he says, "a lot better. You didn't have to go so far and you could fish where you wanted. There wasn't as much pressure to catch and you didn't have to work as quick. They didn't have the technology we've got now. Anyway, it's my last trip."

"As if we didn't already know that," says Paul Heather.

As he goes to sleep in his bunk with Simo telling a vaguely dirty story, the bobbing, dipping and banking of the waves on the ocean below feel comforting in a strange way. Danny dreams of deep under the waves, far below in the freezing water to the seabed, dark and desolate with the cod swimming in shoals, their eyes pale, blind and white and so cold.

He hears a clanging above him; it is the ship's bell on deck, a dull chime that sings out repeatedly. It is uneasy and urgent in the middle of the night. Danny opens his eyes and sees that Simo has jumped off his bed, and the others are making their way out of the bunkroom door. He sits up, unsure if it's real and then follows. He hears shouting from the deck.

"Calm down!" yells the skipper from where he stands in the wheelhouse above. A message is passed along the line of men in the corridor, whispered, for it is not good to mention such things even on the shore, let alone out at sea. Dworkin turns round to relay the message to the last man, Danny. He wears a half-smile that shows his rotten bottom teeth.

"It's the bosun," he says. "He's had his head bashed in. He's dead."

CHAPTER EIGHT

It's just breaking dawn over the North Sea. At the bottom of the steps, the skipper has removed his cap, he took it off as soon as he saw the dead body.

"Right, Boris," he says to the old man. "With Paul here, get him down the steps and into the hold." Boris shakes his pale face. It's cold outside below the wheelhouse.

"I'm not bloody going near it," he says as he retreats. It's unlucky to have a dead body aboard and it's even more unlucky to touch it. Neither Paul Heather nor Simo will carry the body either, or Greasy Joe or the Rat. Vicky is cooking breakfast so it's Big Mike Heather and Danny who clamber up the steps after the skipper.

In the wheelhouse, face down and crumpled on the floor with his knees up to his chest, is the bosun. His mustard coloured beanie is still tight to his head, and his feet are still in his wellies with his mucky waterproof trousers high around his waist like he wears them. There's not much blood on the white metal floor, but what little there is, has frozen solid under his head. The skipper puts his cap back on now because of the cold, and he takes hold of the wheel as he checks the glass dials in front of him. They'll all be dead if he does not keep steering this ship.

Mike bends down to the body and turns it over. The bosun's face lolls and looks blankly at the roof of the wheelhouse with lifeless eyes. Danny can see there is an enormous cut and bruise on the side of his head and there is red down his front from his smashed up nose. Danny feels fear run up through his legs and into his guts. He does not notice the rise and fall of the waves around him at all.

Mike easily heaves the body up with his hands under the shoulders. Danny takes the feet as they drag him out the door and struggle down the steps. Jim has managed to make his way into the wheelhouse as well and is, ironically, sniffing round the blood the bosun has spilt on the cold floor. The skipper grabs the wire-haired dog by his collar and sets him on the stool where Sparky sits.

"I didn't like the man," he whispers, "but I'm not gonna let you bloody eat him."

Mike and Danny struggle down the little corridor with the body. The lad is sweating and there is a bitter taste in his mouth. It's hard to carry a man at the best of times but when he's dead it's more difficult. The legs loll of their own accord, loose change falls out of his upturned pockets, his glasses clatter to the floor from his shirt. Danny does not see them as he struggles over the ruts in the metal floor, and then feels the lenses splinter and crack as he stands on them with one of his boots. They take the body down into the fish room. It's the first time Danny has been in here. Around them are metal bars that stretch high up into the roof and there is a lot more space in here than anywhere else on the trawler. Mike directs him to set the body into a square section in the corner.

"We'll put him there at the bottom," says Mike. The big Heather brother grabs three wooden boards from the stack at the back of the room and begins to slip them in the metal bars that go up to the ceiling. He forms a box around the bosun's body and moves the man's knees so they are up to his chest, then tucks his head in so he will fit into the square. At the ice store, Mike takes the heavy axe that is pinned to the wall, turns the handle to the door and swings it open. Inside there is a wall of frozen water glimmering in the low lights from the ceiling. He takes two good swings and breaks off hundreds of chunks.

"Put the ice on him," says Mike and points to three shovels hanging up on the wall next to where the axe was. It takes them a few minutes to cover the bosun's body with ice chunks. Then Mike takes some more of the boards and fits them over the body to form a shelf.

"I didn't think the first thing we caught would be the bosun," he says. It does not seem like anything out of the ordinary, what they've done. When the fish start coming in, if they come in after this, they will put them into the shelves right up to the ceiling. The wooden boards stop the fish from getting squashed flat. It's almost a perfect place for a dead body. Boris scurries up behind them with his big, wide eyes.

"Make sure he's dead," he says.

"What do you mean?" says Mike Heather. "Of course he's dead, you plum. He's had his head smashed in and his nose broken."

"You can never be too sure. There was that one fella who died twice. It was on The Kingston in the fifties." Mike Heather takes his shovel into both hands like it's a weapon. Boris does not notice and begins to nosey round the box they have made for the bosun's lifeless body. "He was swept out to sea and they fetched him out the water and put him on ice, just like this. Twenty minutes later they heard him coughing and had to get him out the ice again. They fed him warm tea till he got better."

"How did he die twice then?" asks Mike.

"He went down on the Ross Cleveland in the end."

"He's dead. If you'd had enough guts, you'd have helped me carry him down the steps. Lad here did a better job than you." He nods to Danny who is putting the axe and then his shovel back in the right place.

They follow Boris up the steps to the deck and through the little corridor. The old man stops and points at the loose change on the floor. There are two shillings and a shiny penny and the bosun's glasses.

"Pick them up and throw them overboard, will you, lad?" he asks Danny. He bends over to collect the coins. "Don't put them in your pocket, just sling them over the side.

There's a good lad. It wouldn't be right to keep them."

Out on deck, Danny stands next to big Mike Heather and slings the change and the smashed glasses into the North Sea in one go. He does what he's told. It's easier. Mike is steady and looking out into the breaking morning ahead of them.

"I'd have kept that," he says.

"Doesn't it bother you?" asks Danny. "I mean, you don't believe what Boris does?"

"I do," says the big man. "But the sea will have me if it wants. There's nowt I can do about it. You can spin round three times, carry a caul around your neck in a leather bag, never whistle; but if she decides she wants you," he nods to the swirling ocean ahead of him. "Then you won't escape. Why fight against it?" Like his brother, Mike Heather does not even have a nickname. According to Boris, it's unlucky to sail with your family.

In the galley, it's the first breakfast sitting. The crew eat bread that has come fresh out of the oven. This time, Danny sits next to Mike Heather, who he likes, and he watches the big man load a ridiculous amount of butter and then jam onto his bread before he transfers it to his mouth. Just a few moments ago he was carrying a dead body. The crew members fall into their mugs of tea, and there is the clink of cutlery and the hot, heavy sound of men eating without grace.

Nobody has mentioned the murder.

It's like nothing at all has happened.

Danny does not feel like eating when he thinks about the tall bosun with his face white as a cod. He does not like to think of him down there in the fish room covered with ice where they buried him. Jim is scratching at his metal bowl which Vicky filled with whatever leftovers he gave him.

"You'll have to eat something," says Boris, "lad?"

The skipper stands at the swinging doors to the kitchen. He looks at the crew through his steel blue eyes.

"I'll be reporting this when we get back to dock," he says so everyone can hear. "The bosun was an arsehole, but he didn't deserve what he got, and so, there'll be an investigation when we get back. I know it looks like something bad has happened, but I reckon he hit his head and his face—that's what did his nose in. I've said the same thing to Sparky." He points upwards, the radio operator will be in the wheelhouse steering the ship. The men look round nervously and then back to the skipper. Vicky has his head out of the swinging doors and is listening as well. This is the first time Danny has seen him without a grin. He looks different. Silence descends on the trawlermen as they are forced to think about what has happened. The skipper could tell the office by radio right now, but they all know they would have to turn round and go home. There'd be no fish and no pay.

"Where were you this morning, Dworkin?" asks Paul Heather with his cruel eyes. He has a blunt butter knife in his steady hand.

"I was in my bunk," comes the response from the Geordie. "Where were you?"

"In my bed, next to our kid." He means his brother. Mike was born a year after him, which makes the big man younger.

"Who was on duty?" asks Boris.

"He was," says the skipper. "I was on my way up to relieve him. I found him. He was still warm."

"So, what happened?" asks Vicky.

"He hit his head."

"That's bloody obvious, isn't it?" Simo cannot help his sarcasm. Here it sounds cruel.

"I've seen it before," says Boris. "I was fishing out of Fleetwood in the fifties. One of the deckie learners slipped in the fish room in a swell, hit his head on a handle, and that was the end of him." The old man looks into the past as he tells the story. "I just remember his young wife when the skipper told her, shrieking, she was, on the dockside."

The men can all imagine it.

"Things like this do happen," says Skipper Bird. "But the bosun was a good sailor, he knew his stuff. I don't think he would have slipped and fallen, but he could have. Well, he must have."

Paul Heather points at the Geordie and then at Danny. "The only ones we have never sailed with before, are these two," he says. "The ugly one and the lad. Everyone else, you can be sure of skipper but not these two." Danny feels his throat tighten in terror as Paul Heather looks at him. Here is someone who can deliver more than just a beating.

"You can't say that about me," says Dworkin. "Just because I'm on my own and I don't know you. I'm as honest as the next man, me. I was in my bunk, I swear."

"Do you think this lad would hurt anyone?" asks the skipper. It's a question that nobody needs to answer. They all know young Danny cannot even gut a fish yet, let alone hit a man. "Truth is, all of you had something against the bosun. You all hated him. You told him enough times just like he told you."

"That's the way it works on a ship," says Simo. "We might push it. We push each other. That's just how it is, you know that. None of us would have wanted him dead."

"You hated him as well, skipper," says Paul Heather.

"He wasn't my best friend," he answers. "But like Simo says, I wouldn't want him dead."

"You know what I heard?" Paul Heather seems to have heard a lot of things. The skipper does not nod his head because he knows this mean-eyed fisherman will say what he has to anyway. "I heard that the company were finished with you. We all know. Our last trip was the worst you've ever had. It was the worst trip any of us have ever had as well. Me and our kid made a tenner, a bloody tenner for three weeks at sea." Skipper Bird's eyes harden. "We all know that unless you catch more than two hundred tonnes of fish, this time, you're finished. The bosun knew it too. You'll be black-balled. You'll never work St Andrew's Dock again." Paul Heather is telling the truth. Despite who he is, Skipper Dickie Bird is only as good as his last trip. He has said so to Henry Boyce.

"How would that make me kill the bosun?"

"He's the bad luck, skipper. You know it. The bastard did everything wrong. He told us so. You get rid of him and your luck will change. That's why you offed him." The skipper takes a deep breath at this accusation.

"I didn't kill him. You lads know me, and you know me, Paul. Have I ever been anything but fair with you lot?"

"You're a good skipper," says Boris. "We trust you." The crew does not nod. Greasy Joe looks down. They do trust him and he knows this because none of them say they don't.

"Not that I care, skipper," continues Paul Heather. "I mean, I hated that bosun. As far as I'm concerned, he had it coming. With him out the way, we all get paid more anyway." Paul Heather has a morbid sense of truth, but he's not quite right—the bosun's misses will get his share.

"We have to turn back." It's Greasy Joe with his eyes on the skipper. In any other trawler, he the bosun and the wireless operator would have their own space to talk and eat. The chief engineer should have a lot more respect than he enjoys with these men.

"I'm not turning back," says Boris. "This is my last trip. The skipper has promised me a good haul."

"There's been a murder," says the fat man as he blinks through his thick specs.

"I'm not turning back either, Windows," says Mike Heather. "We're already here."

"Calm down, lads," says the skipper with his hands held outwards. "Joe, what difference is it gonna make if we turn back now? We'll keep his body as we have done already.

Mike and the lad have set him in ice. He'll be the same when we get back." Joe shakes his head.

"It's not right though, skipper. I mean someone in this room, or Sparky up in the wheelhouse, one of us has done him in. How's it gonna be, fishing out in the Great North when we know there's someone on this ship could come up behind us and bash us on the head?"

"Nobody bashed him on the head," says the skipper. "This isn't an Agatha Christie film on a Sunday night and nobody is going to hurt you, Joe, are they? Without you, we can't keep that engine going and then we'll never get back home, and anyway… lads, he fell." Joe puts his hand to his head to feel his temple where a killer might have clobbered the bosun. "So, we're not turning back. We keep on. Keep your eyes open."

Paul Heather does a nasty grin and winks at Dworkin before he nods at Danny. "I'm happy with that," he says. Mike Heather grunts in agreement, so does Simo. Greasy Joe shrugs his shoulders in acceptance, he speaks for the Rat as well. Vicky nods and goes back in the little kitchen. Boris sighs.

"What about you, lad?" says the skipper. Danny looks white with fear and shock. The skipper wonders if the boy will ever sail again, after this. Probably.

"I don't have a choice, do I?" It's more than Danny has said to the lads so far as a group. They are wise words. Mike Heather, the most fatalistic of them all, nods in more agreement than he did before.

There really is no choice.

CHAPTER NINE

The skipper asks Danny to get a bucket of warm water from the kitchen and bring it up to the wheelhouse with a mop. Vicky gives him some detergent to put in the water, and he helps Danny take it up, through the ship and to the wheelhouse. The weather is not rough. Though Danny cannot now see anything but the sea in any direction, he doesn't feel as bad as when he could see the coast and feel the strong waves. It seems like it's the afternoon as Danny begins to mop up the bosun's blood from the metal floor, but when he looks at the clock, it reads twenty past nine in the morning.

It's not a good job, mopping the steel floor and the hot water brings a fresh, animal smell to the little room. The skipper watches Danny struggle a little before Sparky stands up and offers to help him.

"Let him do it, Mr Sparks," says the skipper. "He doesn't have much else to do." The man with the brill-creamed head follows his orders and sits back down. He puts his ear to the radio once more. Static rings from the wireless box, it's shrill and lonely.

"Have you heard anything?" asks the skipper. "Are they still at Top Hat?"

"Nothing since last night and it was just chit chat then. The weather isn't looking good. From what I could gather, the boats that are already up there are taking a battering." The skipper nods.

"Good," he says. It's not uncommon for seamen to wish badly on their rivals. They don't want them dead at the bottom of the sea, they just want their fish. "Which way is it heading? The storm, I mean."

"I'll listen at 10 when they do the weather forecast. As long as it's not south."

"It'll be south," says the skipper. You expect the worst so

that you can be happily wrong or if you are right, then you knew it all along.

"Any Russian stuff?" the skipper asks. At times, wireless operators can hear them yapping to each other across the airwaves, submarines talking to ships or base. Sparky looks back at him with nervous eyes.

"I try not to listen, to be honest, skipper."

"The best thing to do," he agrees.

Danny has nearly finished mopping up the blood and is drying the floor with a rag on the end of the brush.

"When you've done that," says the skipper, "tip the bucket over the side and get back in here. You can call your mam." Danny steps into the wind outside, struggles down the ladder, and flings the bloody water into the sea. He looks out across the waves and the grey, dark clouds in the direction the boat is going. He hasn't given his mam or dad a thought this morning. As he climbs the steps to the wheelhouse, he feels a sense of dread; the prospect of talking to his mother is not something he really feels good about doing. Inside and stood behind the skipper, he pipes up:

"I think I'll leave that phone call, Sparky," he says. He blinks. Sparky turns to him with concern.

"You sure?"

"Aye, she won't want to talk to me anyway. I know my mam." Danny does not want this to be true, but he has to face up to it.

"She will want to talk to you," says the skipper. "Give Sparky your mam's phone number, and you'll call her. Don't tell her what's gone on though, best keep that for when we get back home." The skipper means the dead man's blood Danny has just mopped up and the body he and big Mike Heather covered with ice in the fish room.

"She's not bothered, skipper." Danny is surprised he's said this. He wouldn't typically answer or comment to anyone in authority but there's something different about

Skipper Bird, like you can trust him.

"I'm telling you, lad, any mam wants to talk to her son. She's had you in her stomach for nine months for one thing, and then there's the neighbours. What street are you from, again, son?"

"Woodcock Street." A road that runs parallel with Hessle Road itself and is crammed with two up two down terraces. Everyone knows everyone and the neighbours will be aware Danny has gone, they will look to see how his mother acts about it. They will judge her on the way she behaves. It has implications for the skipper also. What will the company think of him if he does not look after his deckie learner? More importantly, what will he think of himself? "She'll be worried sick, whatever you think." Danny nods. He's been told. Sparky contacts Wick Radio—a station far at the northern tip of Scotland. Here the operators will dial up a number on the mainland telephone network and connect it to the ship. Wick Radio is the last point of communication to the rest of the world and they know how to charge. Sparky gives the number to the Scotsman radio operator and hands Danny the Bakelite telephone receiver. The lad holds it to his ear.

The phone rings on the other end. Quarter to ten in the morning on Tuesday. His father will be in bed sleeping after the night shift and his mam will be doing their laundry. Danny can see his little front room now, with the heavy net curtains up to stop people looking in, the telly in its wooden box, the antique patterned settee, and dark green cushions. He can see his dad rolling over in his white bedsheets and cursing whoever would ring so bloody early. Someone picks up on the other end. It's his mam.

"Hello. The Green residence." Her overly formal voice crackles on the airways nearly two thousand miles away across the cold ocean.

"It's me. It's Danny." There comes the silence expected,

and he hears a sniff on the other end and a panting. She is weeping.

"Are you alright, Danny? Tell me you're alright." He has never heard concern in his mother's voice before, and he never realised he had been anything other than a hindrance to her. He expected a barrage of abuse.

"I'm alright, Mam. I'm on a trawler."

"I know, a taxi driver said he saw you. Are you safe?"

"I'm fine. The lads are really nice, and the food's good too. They've got a ship's dog called Jim. I've got a bunk and my own stuff. We'll get to the fishing grounds tomorrow." The words spill quickly out of Danny's mouth.

"Oh, Danny. I wished you'd have told me. I've been so worried. You know what happens to fishermen. It was only last year the Gaul went down. 36 men killed. Danny, you are safe, aren't you, love?"

"We're fine. We've got the best skipper in Hull. Dickie Bird and one of the best trawlers for her size called the Cuckoo." This isn't really true. The ship has seen much better days. Sidewinders aren't that safe either.

"It's good to hear your voice, Danny." The line crackles. "Are you still there?"

"Aye, how's my dad?"

"He's livid with you." Her voice is full of concern. "He's worried as well. You know how he is. He doesn't show it like we do." Sparky taps the face of his watch so Danny can see. His time is almost up.

"I have to go, Mam. I only get a few minutes."

"Alright, Danny... Danny, I love you." It sounds like she is beginning to cry again as Sparky disconnects the call. Slowly, the lad passes back the black telephone mouthpiece, and his face is red with emotion. A tear has caught in the corner of his eyes and it runs down his face.

"Thanks, Sparky," he says, then: "Thank you, skipper." Both men give short bobs of their heads. The weather outside is turning colder, and the clouds look darker in the wide sky in front.

When the lad has left, Sparky says:

"I thought he was going to cry."

"I nearly did myself," answers the skipper.

It's just after two o'clock in the afternoon when the storm really hits. It started heavily raining an hour earlier, a mixture of freezing water and sleet hammered the deck and the little round windows of the wheelhouse. The wind has picked up and so have the waves. If Danny thought he had got used to the rough sea—he was wrong. He has yet to experience the full fury of the north water. The boat drops thirty-foot straight down before sweeping back upwards and over the huge waves. The trawler rolls to one side and then back to the other. Skipper Bird pulls his cap down so it is just over his eyes and glares out through the little storm window at the front, the circular one that spins on a motor so it won't ever freeze up solid like the others. He stands as the boat drops again, feels his legs brace and then watches as the waves crash over the front of the trawler. The bow of the ship has a raised hump deck for this very reason, so the sea can break over it, and the engine powers them back up a wall of water. Sparky leans forward and taps the gyrocompass to make sure it isn't fogged up. The green on the radar bleeps below them. In fog or rain like this, it is impossible to see where you are going, the compass tells the skipper the direction and the radar will tell him if he's about to smash into anything.

"Thank God we've got all this lot," says Sparky as he looks down at the radar. He was a trawlerman for a few seasons in his twenties and then went off to work in the offices for a time. Sparky was also opening batsman for the Marr Fish cricket team and was even scouted by Yorkshire, but there was never any money in it so he got his wireless operator's ticket and went back to sea and off the deck. Since the triple trawler tragedies of 1968, all trawlers must have a wireless man on board and it's not a bad job.

"Remember on the steam trawlers," says the skipper. "We had to carry a hold full of coal to get us out to sea, and there was no radar. None of this radio neither." Sparky shakes his head. He's glad they aren't at the total mercy of the sea like they were back then. "I wouldn't get too full of yourself, Sparky, even with all this technology. The Gaul had all this as well." It only takes one flick of the sea dragon's tail, after all.

It begins to snow and is like dusk outside. The grey clouds pump white, frozen clumps into the sea below, and the wind drives it horizontal. This is bad for many reasons. Snow sticks and freezes. It screws up the radar on the roof of the wheelhouse and, in a few minutes, the Cuckoo is sailing through the North Sea, blind. The green light display of the radar flashes without a signal. They are just like the steam trawlers that went before, or the sailing ships before that, or the wooden merchant vessels or the Viking longships.

It does not take long to show Danny how to play cribbage. There are four of them at it on the table in the bunk room. Boris has explained the rules to the deckie learner and opposite them are Mike Heather and his elder but smaller brother, Paul. Boris is an old hand at the game and fills the thinking spaces with tuts and sighs. Mike looks confused at the cards which seem small in his hands. Paul's face is down, concentrating on his cards, and Danny can see a long slice in the top of his head where his shaven hair does not grow at all.

"Big scar that, isn't it?" says Boris as he sees Danny examining the old wound on Paul's head. The man looks up.

"I'm not telling the story again, Boris."

"It was The Silver Cod, wasn't it?"

"Aye. Some bastard smashed a pint glass over my head." Boris nods at this. They all try not to notice the swells and drops of the boat as they sit playing cards. Danny reaches out to grab onto a bunk as the ship rocks heavily to the starboard. The Geordie lays with his face towards the wall, and the Rat is having a kip with his arm across his face.

"She's pissed off today," comments Simo from his bunk. Danny thinks he means the sea, but he's not sure.

"You did time for it, didn't you? The both of you?" It's Boris again, trying to get the story out of Paul Heather to tell Danny. It's not clear whether the old man wants to frighten the young lad or educate him or perhaps both, to amuse himself, of course.

"You know what happened," cuts in Mike. He turns his face to Danny and explains as a no-nonsense man would, without any of the embellishments or grandeur that might make the story better to hear.

"We had a fight in The Silver Cod. I got six months, and Paul got a year because he knifed someone." Danny nods. Paul Heather does not seem to notice and plays his hand to collect more points. He adds another stick to the cribbage board. It's not right for a man to boast about anything good or bad that he has done. Men akin to Paul Heather from the banks of the Thames or fisherman from Devon or The Mersey may go into great detail about their time in prison or their exploits, but it's not the tradition of these Hull men. Boasting makes people notice you, and you don't want that. You don't want the eyes of the North Sea to notice you. She might want you.

Paul Heather is the kind of man who was naturally good at being in prison. He can fight without being noticed, is able to steal well, knows how to wind someone up and calm them down. He has a nasty charm that can get people to do things for him. More importantly, he doesn't care what others think, unlike his brother, Mike, who did not do so well. The big man has an innate sense of right and wrong and so, should anyone upset him or anyone he likes, he will flatten them.

This is why the three months Mike got for defending his brother in a brawl in a pub on Anlaby Road turned into four months and then six. The big man is also hugely loyal and has been since his mam asked him, before she died, to look after his brother. He has been doing that ever since. They don't hate each other like Boris thinks, they just haven't got anything to say.

Boris places his cards down and grins as he collects more little sticks.

"You got a bird then?" It's Simo from the bunk. He's asking Danny. He means girlfriend. He's fairly certain the lad won't have.

"No," he answers.

"When I was your age," begins Boris. "I was at it morning and night, me. I had a lass on Havelock Street called Stella and one off Flinton Street, she was a posh one." This is far from the truth. Back in 1926, when Boris was the same age as Danny, he had never spoken to a girl apart from his sister. They terrified him and enthralled him in equal measure. "I was up and down Hessle Road, I was. Like a bloody rabbit." He is not boasting because they all know it is not true. Boris will never tell you about his eldest daughter, who, even as the trawler bobs in the storm, sits in a lecture hall at Leeds University in her third year of a chemistry degree. He will never tell what really happened to him during the war, or the reason he has a distinguished service medal with King George embossed on it in his bedside draw at home.

Danny places his cards down and scores fewer points than he would if he were a better player. The trawler drops massively and rocks to one side more severely than it has done previously. Danny glances at Mike Heather with a concerned face and he can see, for the first time, a look of worry on the big man, if only for a second.

"I've got a bad feeling," says Dworkin in his sing-song

voice. "Hitting a storm like this before we even get to the fishing grounds. It's like someone or something doesn't want us to get anywhere."

"You should be careful what you wish for," says Paul Heather, he does not like the Geordie. "You'll be in the nick by the time you get back for doing that bosun."

"I've done nowt wrong," says Dworkin, suddenly sitting up. "And I don't like you saying I have." Paul Heather shakes his head like he shakes off insults. It's easy to wind the Geordie up. He'll remember that. Mike Heather wafts his hand in front of his face as if there is a worse smell in there than the stink of men.

"It's that bloody dog again," he complains. He reaches out and moves Jim, who is sleeping on the end of the Rat's bunk. Jim eats so much fish that he produces powerful bad smells for a little dog, and he lands on his paws. The ship banks again and then dips. Simo swings his legs over his bunk and drops down.

"I need the lav," he announces.

The storm eases into the afternoon. The snow clears up and then turns back to wet rain. The skipper doesn't dare climb on the roof of the wheelhouse to clean off the radar, and he's lucky when the rain washes off the snow. He keeps a check on the temperature outside and on the ice that has frozen up the windows in the wheelhouse. It's bitterly cold.

He looks outside. It's like coming down on a winter's morning and finding a thick layer of snow on everything, only this is ice. The trawl winch line is thick with it, the bars of the rails are triple the size with icicles frozen at an angle. The sea is a lot calmer, but each time the waves break over the Cuckoo, the seawater hits the metal, sticks, and then freezes. It doesn't take long for a build-up like this to make a ship heavier than it should be. It's called black ice, and if it gets bad enough the boat will tip over. It hardly looks real and the skipper is thankful he does not have to change direction. If he did, she might keel over into the water. He rechecks the ice outside. If the bosun were here he would double-check his decision, but he's on his own now.

"Sparky," he says. "Nip down and tell the lads to get their waterproofs on, will you?" The wireless operator nods. That will mean him as well. "We have to get out there and chip off that ice."

A lot of skippers will sit in the wheelhouse all day. They'll give the worst jobs to the lads, have their own cabin, get paid a lot more and pretend it's the right thing because they know more about the sea or that they know how to fill in the official paperwork. They'll also tell you they have the responsibility for the lives of the lads and the ship, and that they carry the can if all goes belly up. It's convenient for some skippers even if it is true.

Standing next to Danny and with a crocodile toothed spanner in his hand, the skipper cracks off the ice from the metal winch cable above him with two big blows. The wind is fierce and the cold is painful. Danny shivers as he watches.

"You have to hit it with a bit of force," shouts the man. Like the skipper, Danny is wearing his full waterproofs. He has the long coat over yellow trousers and rubber boots as well as a waterproof hat on his head on top of a woolly beanie. It is perhaps minus five outside. Danny begins chipping. They are all at it. Boris, Simo, the Heather brothers, even Greasy Joe and the Rat are out in the gale and the ocean spray. Sparky is back in the wheelhouse, but they will take turns. It's horrible in the wind. Danny can hardly breathe, and even though his hands are in rubber gloves they feel frozen.

Fifty quid.

He'd rather not have the money.

CHAPTER TEN

As it's early morning, Jim sits outside the kitchen, just behind the swing doors. He is waiting for his breakfast, but he must be careful. If he enters, Vicky will shout at him, and Jim does not like to be shouted at. He's only allowed in the kitchen when Vicky has dropped something he can't be bothered to clean up, like an egg, which Jim will eat.

Danny watches Mike Heather spread a very thick amount of butter on his bread and cram it into his gob, again. He then takes one big glug of his tea and his Adam's apple bobs as he drains the cup. Vicky passes down a big plate of fried breakfast. Danny has never been given so much food. There are scrambled eggs and bread buns, beans, and tinned tomatoes, mushrooms, chips and hash browns. They need it because of the chipping they did last night, a few hours after they had done it once, the skipper got them all up to do it again.

If Danny had thought travelling on a trawler was unpleasant before, mixed with heavy graft, he now knows some of the true extent of the job. He has also heard from the lads that they have arrived at Top Hat and are going to cast off. The skipper and Sparky have fired the electronic depth sounder and read the printout, they have seen the line of black just off the seabed, and it's not too high. It means there are fish. Danny picks delicately at the plate that has been passed to him. He feels sick.

"You'd better eat that up, lad," says Simo. "You'll need it alright later on."

Vicky comes to the swing doors from the kitchen and shouts over the second serving of breakfast.

"Have any of you lot been in my kitchen?" he yells. There is no answer. Jim looks up at him expectantly and cannot control a little squeak for his breakfast. Nobody answers. "It's just that I could have sworn I left some fish out from yesterday, on the top here, and this morning it was gone. I don't care, I just wanna know." The crew continue eating with scraping on tin plates and the odd belch.

"It'll be the dog," says Paul Heather. Vicky shakes his head.

"He can't get up on the shelf here. It must be me. I must be losing it." Jim gives another yelp for attention, and Vicky gets his bowl full of leftovers and sets it down in front of him. The dog eats with only a little less ferocity than Mike Heather. Vicky stands just behind the swing doors again. "I'm missing tins of fruit as well," he says. This time, not even Jim is listening to him. The dog has finished its food and does not need Vicky until it is just before tea when he gets fed again. Danny struggles to eat. It's too early, and Mike Heather looks down at the lad's plate.

"Are you gonna finish that?" he asks. Danny shakes his head and looks queasy. Mike goes to take the food with one of his big paws and then stops. It's as if something has got the better of him.

"You'll have to get that down you, son. I promise. You'll need it later." Despite his appearance, Mike has emotional intelligence. He can sense the uneasiness in the lad and it makes him feel uneasy as well. It comes from his mother and from looking after his smaller but older brother. Danny puts a fork in the fish and eats it. It's not an order from the big fisherman, more like advice. Danny finds he can eat once he gets started.

Vicky stands at the swing doors again. He is not an aggressive man and so any attempt to be so, only makes the crew more ignorant of him.

"Now I'm missing milk. Are you sure none of you have been in here while I was asleep? I don't even care, I just want to know." There is no reply at all, so he goes back to the stove.

Jim has taken up another position now he has eaten his

breakfast. He sits under Mike Heather's table in case any bits of food fall off. This is important in many ways, anything Jim eats Vicky will not have to clean up, rats won't come looking for it either. There's nothing on a trawler that isn't useful, and this includes Jim. He is a companion who doesn't say anything or pass judgement and also, someone you can show affection to without looking like you're soft. The bosun did not understand this. You cannot always set down how the world works in lists and rules. Dworkin looks at the long-haired Jack Russell with his wonky, eerie eye.

"We normally have ship's cats on Tyneside," he moans. "There's nothing luckier than a cat on a boat." Boris disagrees with this and shakes his head while he chews.

"I used to sail with a lad from Flinton Street," he says. The names of the roads near the dock mean nothing to Dworkin but they are etched with significance to the other lads. Flinton Street is slightly more upmarket than the other terraces. Boris continues, "he always took a cat to sea with him, it was a tabby called Chancer." Dworkin nods at this as evidence that his superstition is correct. "I sailed with him for the best part of twenty years. He never went overboard, never got injured. He was never sick as far as I know and always a happy lad, everyone liked him too."

"That's cats for you," says Dworkin.

Boris has him.

"One night it climbed up a big tree just off Newland Avenue and wouldn't come down, so my mate clambered up to get it and slipped off one of the branches near the top. It took him a week to die. The doctors said he had a slow bleed on his brain. The cat was alright though, as I recall, it lived with his misses for many years to come. Lucky cat that Chancer." Dworkin gives a half snarl. It's not that these men dislike outsiders, it's just Dworkin has done very little to get involved with them. All of his stories are designed to show how much better his experiences are than theirs, how wonderful Tyneside is and how Hull itself is an awful hole.

Outside, it feels like noon but is actually about seven in the morning, and the light is grey as Danny stands in his waterproofs looking at the trawl winch and the cables glistening. The sea around them is glassy smooth and cold. It seems like a different world from the one they were in the night previous. Tiny islands of ice form patterns in the sea around them and it is flat; so flat and calm that it might be the paddling pool in Pickering Park on a winter's day.

The crew have got the net ready. They lift it using the winch, rest it on the side of the trawler and then they let it drop, languid into the water while Simo, Mike and Paul Heather feed the rest of it in. The heavy bobbins clang as they hit the side, they will hold the whole thing on the bottom of the ocean. It takes a few minutes for the trawl to go over. There are headcans, filled with air that will keep the top of the net open under the water and finally, Paul and Mike Heather manoeuvre the otter board into place and drop that in too, this will hold the mouth of the trawl net open as it drags the ocean floor. They all watch as it goes down and the wheels on the winch uncoil the warp cables that stretch to the ocean bed. Danny watches them roll for a long time. He doesn't like to think about how deep the bottom of the sea may be, it gives him a sensation of being very high up. The water around them returns to being glassy smooth once more with just the warp cables trailing down into the cold. Boris lights up a cig. The skipper telegraphs the order, and down in the engine room, Greasy Joe turns the dial and the propellers spin in the ocean behind. The Cuckoo rumbles and begins to move off.

"What now?" asks Danny.

"Usually about two hours. Depends on how the skipper feels," says Boris. "Then all the fun starts." The old man takes a big pull on the cigarette and smoke comes out of his nose. Danny walks to the side of the trawler. It's like being on another planet and he looks at the crew with understanding. They are far away from Hessle Road here, in the still and patchy mist of the Arctic waters, in silence. Like ancient hunters, they have travelled to a dangerous place where they are not meant to be. Danny's back prickles with the fear of what may be coming.

Dworkin walks onto the deck with his limp. He does a series of rough coughs without covering his mouth and Paul Heather shoots him a nasty look. Mike Heather inspects the winch and the warp cable, he doesn't want it to snap. Greasy Joe has oiled it already and the motor purrs as it uncoils. Paul Heather rolls himself a cigarette in paper. Dworkin coughs again like an invalid. He looks pathetic as he leans against the trawl winch.

"We once caught a whale in a trawl," says Boris.

"Not this one, again," says Simo.

"It's good for the lad," says the old man. His eyes flash as he carries on. "It was a humpback, must have been a young un to get caught in the trawl. It had its head stuck right in the cod end of the net, that's the little end, lad. It took about ten of us to get it on the boat, and we had to cut it out with our knives. It was a big beast of a fish and one of its big eyes looked at me as it lay there on deck. We couldn't lift it back in so the skipper ordered us to take axes to it. It were horrible, a right job, with blood and blubber all over as we cut chunks off it and threw them back in the sea. It kept looking at me that whale did, and I felt sorry for it." Boris looks back in time again, at the deck of the steamer trawler all those years ago and the whale fish they butchered down to its bones. He is left with his own thoughts and the men listening wish they had not heard it. None of the men are here to hurt anything, apart from Paul Heather maybe, and the death of such a creature is nothing to be happy about.

"Can we have some music on?" shouts Paul Heather up at Sparky in the wheelhouse. The man nods.

"Aye," says Boris. Sound might wash away the memories. Sparky hits the switch and music blasts out of the cans onto the deck. It's a swing tune from the fifties. Boris smiles at this. Paul Heather waves up at Sparky,

"Can we have another station? We don't want all this old stuff." Sparky opens the window.

"It's the only one I can get lads, we're too far north. It's American Services Radio, unless you want something in Norwegian." Paul Heather pats his hand in the air as if swatting the idea away.

"Not that rubbish," he says.

Somewhere, deep on the ocean floor behind them is the trawl net. Its mouth is open in the darkness like a huge man-made whale; already, the slippery, silver cod, haddock and mighty halibut are being swept up and into it.

Danny can't stop thinking about the bosun, lifeless in the fish room with his eyes wide.

It's the waiting time. The Heather brothers stay on deck to keep a careful eye on the winch as they smoke. They watch the lines and the wheel. If the cables go tight then the net has got snagged on something down below. They have to be careful too, warp cables can be wild and nasty when they break. But today it's not so bad. At least the weather is good and the sea is calm even if it's still deathly cold.

Simo goes back to reading his book on Elvis Presley. The sailor played bass in a rock and roll outfit in the sixties called The Kestrels. They once supported The Small Faces at Bailey's in Bond Street. In 1969, three months after they got married, Simo's wife told him she was pregnant and it was either the bass or her. He put the bass in the loft in its expensive case and never played again. She left him a year later for a haulage firm owner from Doncaster and Simo moved back in with his mam. Then he needed money and to get away from her, so he joined the trawlers. It was a lot like being on the road in a band with the same banter, just without the music.

Sparky pipes American forces radio around the ship and they listen to Everybody was Kung Fu Fighting which Danny likes. Boris does not approve of this new music and says so often. The skipper stands at the stern of the boat with little Jim next to him and they watch the smooth, shiny ocean and the steel cables that run down into the dark water. He scratches his beard as Danny comes up behind him. The skipper turns to the lad.

"What do you think, son?" Danny does not know what he is being asked. "Do you think it's time to pull up the net?" Danny doesn't know what to say. Nobody ever asks his opinion and it seems like the decision to pull up the net is a big one. A lot of the trawling game is luck after all. It's been about an hour and a half since they dropped it. Danny squats down and fusses Jim behind his ears.

"What do you think, Jim?" he asks the little dog who cocks his head to one side as Danny scratches it. "I reckon we should see what we've got," he says.

"So do I," replies the skipper. "Let's bring her up."

It's all hands on deck. Boris is the winchman. He has to pull the lever slowly, and if the warp cable complains too much, he has to ease off. They might be pulling up tonnes of fish, who's to know. The rest stand round nervously with their breath making billows of steam in the cold, late morning, waiting for the net to break the surface of the water. Despite the calm, there is danger here, still. Boris has seen a winch cable snap, whip back and nearly cut a man in half. On his first trip, he got his arm trapped in one and has the scars to show for it like a road map up his left bicep and shoulder. He goes steady, bringing the whole thing up from the depths as slowly as he can. Mike Heather watches with his foot on the side of the trawler, leaning on his knee. He sees the top of the net break the surface, then the rest of the trawl, full of shiny silver fish, wriggling and slapping at each other but held tight by the crisscrossed chords.

"There's the green," he yells out at the water as he points. It's ironic that this is the name they give to the fish they want so badly. They drag the trawl towards the ship in the calm water and then winch it on board, bit by bit. It's a big job. The sidewinder dips to the side at the weight, and Danny looks nervously at the skipper in the wheelhouse. It feels like they might go over with the load but none of the crew seem concerned. Gulls fly down with squawks and pick at the top. It's like a colossal sock, full of wriggling fish and tied at one end. When they eventually get the trawl net onto the boat, Paul Heather goes to the rear of it and undoes the cod end. Silver fish spill out, thousands of them, flapping and slapping at the deck as they struggle to breathe with their gills opening and closing. Boris uses the winch to pull the trawl up further, and they empty all the fish from the rest of the net. They are mostly cod and, in the middle, there is an exceptionally large flatfish, dark brown on top with a white belly. It's almost as long as Simo is tall. A halibut. There are smaller fish and eel-like creatures, blobs of stuff and bits that don't look like anything animal. There are some strange things on the bottom of the deep sea. The catch smells strong, and the salt burns Danny's eyes. Dworkin and Boris begin to reset the net while the others deal with the fish, the Geordie does know what he's doing, but he's slower than Boris. Paul Heather watches as the goggle-eyed man struggles with the weight of it on his gammy leg. He tuts.

"Deckie Learner," says Mike, "here," he beckons and Danny wades through the fish in his oversized boots on his oversized feet. Mike Heather must teach him correctly because if the deckie learner knows how to gut quickly and where to throw the liver and the fish, Mike will get through these thousand in less time. He will get his money more rapidly, and he will be home more quickly to see the fat lass from St Georges Road who he likes because she makes him laugh. Mike is a good teacher; he shows as he was shown. First, Danny watches him reach down and collect a cod, cut a slice in the belly, find the liver, pull it out and then throw it in the bucket Simo has set in the corner. These are valuable. He then opens the creature up more and removes the guts which he tosses overboard.

Paul has turned on the fish washer on the opposite side of the boat, and this is where Mike chucks the rest of the fish. Danny watches him do it three or four times before Mike makes him try it, while the big man watches him. Danny is clumsy at first, he has only used a knife to peel potatoes before but he is a trier and does not want to let the other lads down. Mike appreciates this. When he is sure the lad can do it, he begins to cut and gut more fish himself.

"Do that for the next eight hours, and we'll be done."

The work is hard.

Danny's hands swell up inside the rubber gloves. The sea gets rougher around them, and they get covered in spray as they gut the fish and throw them in the washer. After an hour of cutting, it does not seem like they have even made a dent in the number of fish on the deck and Danny feels faint. It has been a good haul to start with, if they keep this up, they will soon fill up the fish room.

Sparky comes to help cut the fish as the waves get worse. The wind whips up. Before he knows it, Danny is struggling to keep his footing on the slippery deck as the boat rocks on the heavy sea. Water washes over the side and drenches him in freezing ice slurry, it goes over the sides of his boots and into his socks and down the neck of his waterproof jacket. The lad goes ridged with shock at the cold, and the trawler rolls forward, suddenly going down a steep bank of water and then just as quickly, back up once more. These are bigger waves than they have seen for a few days. They have come out of nowhere. If it gets too bad, the skipper will order them off deck but he'd rather not do this, nobody wants to lose any fish back into the sea from where they have come.

Up in the wheelhouse, the skipper sees another wave coming towards them perhaps thirty seconds away. They will drop into it and the sea will bust over the bow of the ship with a force that the fishermen need to be aware of. Skipper Bird sees Danny at the port side of the trawler, next to the railings and struggling to keep his feet. There's Boris near the winch and Mike Heather behind him. Simo is on the other side of the fish washer. The lad looks vulnerable suddenly and the skipper wonders why he talked him into joining the crew back in Hull. They could have still landed the same amount of fish without him, probably. There at the side of the boat with his back to the sea with no knowledge of how to stand or what to do, the lad is in more danger than he can know. When the wave breaks and the deckie learner is not ready for it, he could be knocked to the deck and smash his head. If the boat dips to the side when the wave hits, he will be washed off. The skipper makes for the window and flings it open, yelling at the fisherman working on deck.

"Hold on, fellas!" he shouts as loud as he can. Mike Heather has his leg around a post. Dworkin is steady nearer the wheelhouse, Boris is tucked in next to the fish washer, Paul Heather is down in the fish room and will be packing the fish away. Danny is too confused to know what is going on. He has only just got used to the feeling of the waves and is standing in totally the wrong place.

This is how tragedy happens.

It's swift, cruel, and without warning. The skipper shouts again at Danny, but the boy does not look up as the boat goes upwards over the wave.

It's so quick.

The bow of the trawler dips sharply, and the wave crashes

onto it and over the front, sending seawater high and above the crew's heads. The port side pitches down, exactly how the skipper did not want it to, and he looks on in horror as the sea collects the lad from the deck. It grabs him and flips him backwards over the rail, and his yellow boots go over into the sea. The skipper feels his heart drop as the boat rocks to the other side.

She's got him.

The skipper is at the window again and yelling. His mind races. He sees himself sat on his bunk later on after half a bottle of scotch with his face in his hands and silent tears pouring through his fingers. He sees the face of Danny's mam as he explains what has happened, listens to the man from the company tell him Danny should not have been aboard the ship at all because he did not sign the correct documents.

It has taken just one second for him to go.

A heartbeat.

The skipper roars at the lads.

"Man overboard!" He can see Boris and Mike Heather running to the place where Danny has been swept over but there is no sign of him. In a sea like this, he'll be gone. For a few helpless moments, the men look out to the ocean and each other. The boat rocks and another wave bashes the side again. Mike Heather and Boris grab onto the railing to keep from being swept off themselves and fish tumble over the side. The skipper must get back to the wheel or they could spin round. As another wave breaks over the side of the Cuckoo, he sees Danny, still wearing his long jacket but without his hat as he is washed back onto the deck and into the pile of fish.

She's given him back.

The skipper has heard it so many times: a trawlerman washed overboard and then washed back on deck again as if he were not quite to the taste of the ocean. It's a folk tale every fishwife on St Andrew's Dock knows, every hairdresser, taxi-driver, fish factory filleter, bobber, shipwright or clerk will tell it to you as a joke, but here it is. Mike Heather scrambles for the lad and picks him up by the waist of his trousers, there's a line of blood along his temple where he has hit his head. The big man yells at Danny to see if he is still alive and sets him on his feet. He's as white as snow as he walks to the accommodation below the wheelhouse.

"Grab the wheel, Sparks," says the skipper as he races to the door and climbs down the metal steps. On deck, he reaches out to the deckie learner, grabs him by his collar and pulls him close. Two minutes earlier, this boy was in the Barents Sea, and the skipper could cry with happiness as he looks into this tall lad's watery red eyes and pale face.

"You're bloody lucky," he yells against the wind as he holds him. It would have broken the skipper to lose anybody, especially this one. His grip is strong on the collar. "Are you alright, lad?" The boy nods. Everything that has happened to the skipper in the last few months comes to the front of his mind. He sees his wife, sat on the edge of their armchair in the front room as she tells him she lost the baby, their baby, their first one. The one she had dreamed about for so many years. This lad with his frightened eyes, he could be the skipper's boy in another world; he is someone's boy now, and worth more than all the fish in the whole of the cold sea. Tears form in the skipper's eyes. He has to fight them down and bury them deep like he's been trained to. He must break the tension with something or he will be overcome with emotion, and there is no need for that out here.

"If you want to go swimming, lad," he says as his voice breaks, "do it on your own time."

After he gets changed into dry clothes, the skipper lets Danny steer the boat for the whole afternoon while he cuts fish with the crew. He pops back to check on the wheelhouse every half an hour. The lad is shaken but otherwise okay and the skipper has given him a shot of whiskey, a cup of warm cocoa and half a packet of bourbon biscuits while he steers. They are all relieved.

"I've never been swimming in the sea before," says Mike Heather as he cuts fish. "He's a lucky sod."

"He's a good lad, lucky too," says Boris.

"I've never seen owt like it before," says Simo.

"He's a good sign, that lad is," says Dworkin. It is perhaps the first thing he has said that Mike Heather or Boris agree with.

The trawler floodlights come on at about three when the sun goes down. The men must work through the night. This is not a nine to five job; they are not accountants who go home when the clock says they should. They will go at the job till it is done. The trawler nets do not come up so full and, in the early hours of the morning, the skipper decides it is not worth dropping the trawl for the fourth time; they will move on somewhere new.

The lads have got through a good amount of the fish on deck, and the skipper sends Danny down to the fish room where Paul Heather has been for the last ten hours. It will keep him off deck, at least, and keep everyone from worrying.

In the fish room, Paul Heather has a woolly hat with flaps that cover his ears. He packs the fish level on aluminium trays and builds up the boards around them, so that, where there was an empty room before, there are now three columns of those wooden boards stacked with fish. Paul's face looks red from the cold. He likes to work alone so he scowls at Danny.

"Chip off a load more ice, will you?" he asks. Danny takes the big axe off the wall, opens the ice cupboard door, and starts to swing. He makes a little dent in the ice crystals with an uneducated effort that has too much power in it. Paul Heather stands behind him and watches him work.

"You're one lucky bastard," he says. "I've heard about people getting washed overboard and then getting washed back, but I never thought it would happen." Danny turns and smiles. There's something not quite right about Paul Heather as he gives an evil chuckle. "I saw where you put the bosun, I'd have cut his throat if it were me." He makes it sound like what happened was a good thing. Danny keeps on at the wall of ice. "It was that Dworkin who did it, you know, he was the one. I'll get him on the way back, you'll see. There's no point in getting him now, we need him to work, but once we set sail back to Hull, I'm gonna teach that Geordie bastard a lesson he won't forget. Have you seen him limping round with his leg? What's a man like that doing on a trawler?" Paul Heather steps into the ice room closer to Danny. "You know lad when I do him, I want you well out the way. I want you quiet. I might even ask you to get the skipper to look the other way. You in for that?" Danny is not sure what Paul is asking him or what he plans to do to the Geordie with the gammy eye. He does what his mother always does when she's asked a question she can't answer— ignore it. Paul Heather steps up and pokes him in the back. "I said, are you with me on this?" Danny feels scared.

"Aye," he answers.

"Good." Paul Heather steps back into the fish room. There's been a build-up of cod coming down from above. "Me and our kid like you, lad. We could be mates. Now, shovel some of that ice to the wheelbarrow and bring it over here."

Danny is not sure he wants to be Paul Heather's mate.

They move off Top Hat and up the Kidney Bank, so-called because if you draw a line around the shape of it on the map it looks like a kidney bean. There is still a lot of fish to deal with, and after close to sixteen hours on his feet, Danny has come to understand a new form of pain. Boris has told him and Mike Heather to get something to eat and then go to bed.

Danny sits next to Mike with a vacant look on his face as Vicky sets a plate of fish and chips down in front of him with mushy peas. He now understands why Mike Heather must eat so much and so quickly; he needs fuel to power his massive arms, chest, and legs. They do not speak as they eat, little Jim waits below the table, as he always does. Chips fall off and he deals with them efficiently.

The two men do not speak either, as they walk to the bathroom. Danny goes for a wee in the tin urinal. He looks up into the corner of the room where icicles hang from the ceiling and realises the whole wall is frozen. The boat rocks one way, Danny lightly bangs his head. Mike Heather is brushing his teeth.

"Best get some kip," he says into the tiny mirror. "We'll be up in six hours."

In the bunkroom, Danny yanks his boots off but does not get undressed as he falls into bed. He pulls the covers over him and is asleep before his head touches the pillow. It is the first day of graft he has ever done; he has been washed overboard and back on, his hands are swollen from work, his legs stiff and his feet frozen and sore.

There is fear in his dreams; the nasty eyes of Paul Heather, Dworkin's grin, a gull looking at him from the bow of the ship, the bird tattoo on Boris's leathery hand and a mermaid, deep in the cold ocean with her hair flowing around her.

CHAPTER ELEVEN

Boris shakes Danny awake. It is morning but still dark, and the bunk room stinks of working men's sweat, grease, fish liver and the salty sea. It takes Danny a minute to come to his senses. His hands sting and his body is stiff. For a minute, he dreams he is at home and it's his dad shouting at him to wake him.

"Time to get up, lad," says the old man. He sits down on Danny's bunk. "My turn to kip now. The skipper wants you at breakfast."

Danny manages to pull his boots on. As soon as he stands up, he hears Boris snoring below him. It's not clear what day it is, or what time it is, he does not know where he is for a few more seconds. Danny did not bother to take his clothes off the night before so he does not have to worry about putting them on again. In the darkness, he struggles down the corridor as the ship rocks one way then the other.

Danny sits down alone in the little galley and notices for the first time there's a framed black and white photo screwed to the wall, it's a windmill, must be the one at Skidby. It seems like land is a million miles away. Vicky passes him a plate of fried, but not battered fish with mushy peas, for breakfast. It's just fuel. Vicky looks at him.

"You'll get used to it," he says.

"I'm not complaining," says Danny. This is genuine. Vicky taps the lad on the shoulder. He is learning.

The skipper should have said, fifty quid and as many fish and chip dinners as you can eat.

Danny stands in the wheelhouse behind Sparky and the skipper. Dawn is just breaking around them. The last of the three big hauls are packed away, and the crew are sleeping apart from the three of them in the wheelhouse and big Greasy Joe in the engine room. The radio hisses as Sparky puts it to his ear, the electro gyroscope holds the direction and the radar bleeps. It's peaceful. Sparky lights one of his cigarettes and the smoke goes up Danny's nose.

Danny feels like he has been at sea his whole life with the Cuckoo clapping over the waves on the open ocean. The radio crackles into being and a voice sounds over the cold sea from somewhere in the grey morning.

"Trawler Cuckoo H.142. You are not allowed to fish in these waters. Stop fishing immediately." It's a foreign-sounding accent. Sparky is confused. They are not near Iceland, they are nearer to Norway. There's no reason for them not to be here unless it's the Russians. He looks up at the skipper with a frown. The voice sounds again.

"You are not allowed to fish in these waters. Remove yourself from this area." As if they didn't have enough to worry about with the bosun, the ice and cold, now this. The skipper listens to the voice coming through the static and his mind picks over what it could be. He can't see any ships on the horizon, but that doesn't mean there isn't anyone there; with telescopes you can see a long way. The cod wars have raged for a few years. Icelanders don't want trawlers from the UK in their waters and have tried to impose a 200-mile limit around their island that fisherman are not allowed in. They send gunboats out to scare the trawlermen and cut their trawl lines so they lose their nets. Skipper Bird has had run-ins with them before and he can see their point. He still doesn't like to have guns pointed at him. It's one of the reasons he's going past Bear Island, so he doesn't have to go anywhere near them. The voice comes back again.

"The Cuckoo H.142, do you understand me?" There's something odd about the pronunciation and a smile breaks across the skipper's face.

"It's someone taking the piss," he says.

"You must not fish in these waters," comes the voice again. Danny spots a dot on the horizon a long way off. It's another trawler. The skipper picks up the receiver.

"This is H.142 the Cuckoo. Who's this?"

"It's me, it's Al." The skipper shakes his head. He knows this man. Mucky Alan Coates from Grimsby. A yellow belly and a bastard to boot. His trawler is a sidewinder also, but newer. Like lots of Grimsby trawlers, it has the word Arctic in its name, the skipper thinks this is the Arctic Warrior. He must have binoculars.

"You tosser," answers the skipper.

"I had you there," says the now northern voice on the other side. Sparky rubs his face and sighs.

"Very funny," there is no trace of humour in the skipper's voice. "What do you want?" The skipper doesn't like men from Grimsby in as much as they are rivals and they catch fish that he could catch. Coates also has a reputation for driving his crew too hard.

"I'm on my way back to port now," comes the voice, clear and high through the radio. The trawler is moving towards them from far in the distance. You would think that men in command of big ships in dangerous waters would have more reverence for each other and their situation, but Skipper Bird and Mucky Al Coats here might as well be on home-made rafts and shouting abuse at each other on the boating lake on East Park.

"How much did you catch?"

"Hardly anything," the voice sounds strangely happy. "It's been a bad trip. I've got maybe a ton in the fish room down here. I'm only heading back because I'm out of fuel. How about you and your girl?" It's a lie. His fish room will be full or he would not be returning to dock in Grimsby. Mucky Al Coates is probably drunk already. You cannot get stopped by the police this far out to sea.

"We haven't caught anything yet," answers the skipper. "We're on our way to Bear Island, then we'll shoot." A lie also. Neither man wants to say what he has in his hold for many reasons: Skipper Bird does not want to boast of his catch already, this would be unlucky. Also, he does not want to give Coates any information that may help his fishing in the future.

"I heard you mucked up last time, Birdie," says the voice.

"How so?"

"You came back into port with a quarter of the fish you needed. Sounds like you've lost it to me, mate."

"You believe everything your mam tells you, do you?"

"Mostly aye, especially when it's a cod head skipper who's come unstuck. Makes us happy it does." People from Hull call those south of the Humber yellow bellies, and in turn, they are called cod heads. They don't hate each other but they pretend to.

"It's just jealousy, mate, we can work harder and catch more in a smaller boat." The voice on the other end laughs, it's a smoker's rough cackle.

"You're too soft on your lads, Birdie, way too soft. You've got to show em some steel once in a while, you know, make em fear you."

"You should be working back in them offices with the rest of the silver spoon suits if you think like that. I treat my lads like I'd treat my mates." It's the truth. "I get respect for it too. You can't buy that with all your gold in Grimsby."

"You're a born loser, Birdie. I knew that when I first saw you. A chancer, a dreamer and a loser. The north water's no place for men like you." The banter is good-natured between the two, but there is the sting of truth somewhere behind the words. "This'll be your last job then?"

"Not me. I'll be fishing these waters when you're long gone." The skipper smiles. It's nice for him to have someone poke fun at him. Nobody onboard the Cuckoo would dare.

"I can come aboard for a drop if you've got ten minutes." The skipper thinks about this. He does not have time. He has to get past Bear Island to Kidney Bank as soon as he can. He also has a dead body on board in his fish room, and while there is not a chance this man would find it, Skipper Bird doesn't take risks.

"I'm too busy to stop, mate."

"Well then, if you manage to catch enough and you keep your job, I'll buy you a pint when I see you."

"I'll buy you one," replies the skipper. He sets the receiver down and the radio goes silent.

They watch for the next half an hour as the trawler steams towards them and then The Arctic Warrior comes into view. It has a vivid red bow and a black wheelhouse. It's like they are a mirror image of the Cuckoo, only a brighter version of them, shining in the morning sun. On deck there are two seamen in yellow trousers, waving, and in the round window of the wheelhouse, skipper Al Coates sticks two fingers up at the Cuckoo as she drifts past. He has a black peaked cap and white beard with a big smile. Danny looks back at the wake they are leaving in the smooth sea.

Part of him wishes he were aboard that ship and bound for home.

Simo and Danny are on deck mending nets. It's complicated. Simo explains how to measure out and tie the string with the bobbin pin. Like Mike Heather, he knows if he can get the deckie learner to do the job he would do, it will take him half the time to do it. He watches the lad work and corrects him as he goes.

Paul Heather steps up to the wheelhouse door, opens it and glares inside. The skipper is at the wheel. The rest of the crew are busy. Vicky is in his kitchen. Simo, Danny, and Boris are fixing the nets with Dworkin. Mike Heather is in his bunk. Paul pushes open the door a little further and his cruel eyes see the skipper alone at the wheel.

"You don't have to stand at the door, mate," calls Skipper Bird. "Come in. What's on your mind?" Paul pushes open the door.

"That Geordie," he answers.

"What about him?"

"Lots of things. He can't work."

"Seems to do okay."

Paul Heather tuts. "He's a half-wit and you know as well as I do, it was him involved somehow. I just know it." The skipper turns to this man.

"Involved in what?"

"The bosun's murder. What else?"

"Could have been you." This is the way to deal with Paul Heather. To control the conversation rather than let him tell you what he wants you to think. The man's face screws up with indignation and anger.

"You what? I didn't have anything to do with it!"

"Seems to me, you're so keen to pin the blame on someone else. Why would you do that if you didn't think the finger could be pointed at you?" The skipper is calm.

"I knew the bosun as long as you did."

"You hated him as well."

"So did you."

"You could have bumped him off for all I know," says Paul. The skipper cocks his head at this. "It was you that found him."

"Nobody bumped him off, he fell. It was an accident; they happen at sea. What do you want? Really?" Paul is a little disarmed by this.

"The bosun was an arsehole, but he was a bloody good sailor, he wouldn't just slip like some galley lad. I want you to know that something's not right."

"What?"

"Everything. Running low on diesel, that kid's green socks, what happened to the bosun. It just doesn't feel right." The skipper nods at this. It really doesn't feel right. "And how much fish we caught yesterday, and for it all to dry up in three trawls. It's like she's telling us to go home. She's given us something and we should take that dead body and go back with it. Skipper?"

"I know what you mean." He turns to the wheel and checks the course on the gyrocompass. They are still bound for Bear Island and just north of it, to the fishing ground the skipper feels will be lucky, the Kidney Bank. The trip does feel harder than usual, the weather is worse and the smell of fish fouler, but the skipper cannot turn back. "I'll be finished, Paul, if I don't bring home a decent catch." The skipper knows this will be the end of his seafaring life anyway, he's already promised.

"It might be the end of all of us if we keep going," says Paul Heather.

"That's a chance you took when you stepped on this ship. You know what can happen at sea."

"That's not what I mean, skipper. If someone has killed the bosun, then you could be next."

"He hit his head, it's simple as that."

Paul Heather sighs. "You know, skipper I look after number one, me, and I'll protect myself over anybody, even my brother. Remember that." This is not a new piece of information for the skipper. He knows what kind of a man Paul Heather is.

"Duly noted, mate," answers the skipper. "Close the door on your way out." Paul Heather narrows his eyes at the back of the skipper's head.

"You'll regret not believing me," he says.

"I'm sure I will. Like I said, close the door on your way out." Paul Heather goes down the steps outside, and his boots clang on the metal.

The skipper wipes his forehead and then his eyes. There is something not right about Dworkin but then again, there is something definitely wrong with Paul Heather as well.

Sometime around midday, Bear Island appears out of the fog. It's not much more than a titanic lump of rock sticking out of the water. Boris and Danny stand on deck looking at it in the distance between the grey clouds across the sea.

"There it is," says the old man.

"Are there loads of bears on it?" asks Danny.

"Nope. The Dutch bloke who discovered it saw a polar bear swimming in the water, so they say. That's why it's Bear Island. Nobody lives there. There's nowt on it. What would be the point?" Danny had hoped to see a polar bear, but from this distance, all he can see are stone cliffs with white snow on top of them and tiny dots that are sea birds.

"It's the last time I'll see that," says Boris.

"I hope it's my last as well," says Danny.

"You'll be back once you see the money. We all say that on our first trip. It gets in your blood."

"I thought you hated it."

"Part of me does. Part of me loves it. People from where we come from don't always say what they mean. Trawlermen say they love it and never come back, lads say they hate it and can't get out to sea again quick enough."

"My dad says I should get out of Hull."

"You might as well," says Boris. "I don't know how long they've got left in the fishing business what with the Cod Wars, the Russians, the fisherman from Grimsby, the amount of ships that go down. I don't know how long there is. It isn't like it was when I was your age, that's all gone. One day our way of life will be gone as well." Danny looks at the deep creases and wrinkles in Boris's leathery face, the white eyebrows and the hairs growing out of his nose. A man who has spent his whole life at sea. Danny can see the future frightens him.

"It'll be alright," he says.

"I don't know if it will," answers Boris. "I don't know how I'll get by when I'm at home. You will visit me, won't you lad? Tell me all the stuff that's been going on here on the Cuckoo, won't you?" Danny nods. "I just don't know how I'll be with normal," he continues. "Life's always been too much or too little. Too much fish, too little fish, too much money, too little money, not enough time at home, too much time at home, too much luck, not enough luck. How will it be?" Boris would not speak this way to anyone else, not even his wife. Somehow, Danny's naive wide eyes have made Boris trust him and say things to himself and to the world that he would not ordinarily say.

"It'll be okay," says Danny, again. He does not know what will make this old man feel better. Boris smiles. Just by listening to him, Danny has made him feel better.

"It's just an old fisherman talking crap," he says. "You'll do it yourself if you get to my age."

In an hour, darkness envelops them. This close to the Arctic Circle it's more night than it is day. The cold comes down harder than it has and the deck freezes.

The skipper checks his deep sounding device and reads the printout again. He sees the black line on the bottom of the seabed. Fish. He rings the ships bell at five in the afternoon when it's pitch-black. Time to shoot the trawl.

They wait for four hours before the skipper tells them to haul the net up. In the darkness, it is half full of silvery fish that slap and flap onto the deck as Paul Heather undoes the cod end. Once more, they are surrounded by the wriggling of them and they fall to gutting. It is relentless, the skipper tells them to shoot the nets and then haul them up again. The trawl winch complains at the weight. Under the deck floodlights, they start to haul in big. The number of fish around Danny's wellies swells so he does not really have to bend down to pick one up. He has got quicker at the job as well so he can pull the liver from one nearly half as fast as Paul Heather or Simo. Periodically, the trawler sways to one side, but there is not the bad weather they had previous.

After a few hours, the skipper himself takes a turn on the decks with the lads, and the wind is down so they can hear each other speak. Danny appreciates Skipper Bird; another captain might spend his time in the warm wheelhouse sipping cocoa, but this man wants the job done and so he will lend a hand himself. Paul Heather likes this too. Boris does not care. The dawn is beginning to break over the ocean and the sky turns a pale watery grey but it's still dark enough to need the deck lights. Vicky brings them all out a flask of cocoa which they pass to each other after having a swig. It tastes like heaven and Danny grins as he passes it to Dworkin. He feels happy here in the middle of the Barents Sea in the bitter cold with a job to do and a smile forming on Mike Heather's face. The sun shines on the horizon like a page from the bible, majestic and pale in the distance.

"Have you heard the tale of The Nelly?" asks the skipper. He is talking to Danny. The boy shakes his head. The skipper begins. Boris has heard this one before but likes it, Paul Heather has not and neither has Dworkin. The skipper knows a story is as good a way as any to pass the time, it can make you forget your cold hands and frozen feet. The skipper tells it as he was told it.

"It was 1973 and a hard winter aboard The Nelly, one of the last of the small steamer ships built in the fifties. It sailed out of Hull and made the same trip we're doing, out past Bear Island. The skipper was a hard bastard, a Makem called Stanley. He'd converted the boat from steam to diesel, and they had two big tanks on the ship that they could fill with fuel, and when one of the tanks was empty, they'd fill it with fish. If you've ever smelled diesel, then you'll know that it doesn't go well with anything you eat, so before they could put any fish in the tank, they had to clean it out. It was big enough for a lad to climb into, and on this one trip into the Norwegian Sea they use up the last of the diesel and old

Stanley orders their newest lad, a deckie learner like you, to go down into the tank with soap and rags, and wash the thing out. He's there for an hour or so before this deckie learner begins complaining he can't breathe so well. Stanley goes down to see what all the fuss is about and listens to the young un as he's panting inside. Like I said, Stanley is a hard bastard and he never listens to his crew. He only wants to catch more fish to make more money, so he closes the big lid of the tank and tells the lad inside he can come out when it's all clean." The skipper's voice goes quiet. "Of course, the fumes overcome him in a few minutes and Stanley tells the rest of the crew to ignore his banging. When the bosun opens the big lid, he has to go down the ladder and pull the deckie learner out, he's dead. Stanley, being the skipper he is, can't be bothered to fill in the paperwork or the documentation, so he gets the crew to swear down he was washed overboard, and they throw his body into the sea behind the trawler." The skipper looks up to see Danny's face and eyes, a little fearful as he guts another cod, pulls out the liver and throws it into the bucket.

"Now it turns ugly, see. For the rest of the trip round Bear Island here, the crew keep saying they can see the lad's face in the water looking up at them from the waves. It starts to worry them, even more so, when Stanley himself sees the same face looking at him from the waves formed in the white froth. All the way around the bottom of Svalbard and back home again, the skipper can see the boy, all the way back to Hessle Road and up Boulevard when he gets back home. He sees the lad's face when he's in his tin bath in the kitchen. He sees the kid in his dreams too, hears him banging on the side of the tank when he's in bed. They say on a clear night, you can still see the young deckie learner's face if you look at the waves and you can hear him banging on your hull walls." Danny feels a tingle down his legs in fear. He dare not look back at the ocean in the half-light of the morning, but he does not want to show any fear on his face for the other lads. Somewhere at the bow, Simo cracks the iron trawl winch with a spanner, and it rings out in a low dong around the deck of the ship. Young Danny nearly jumps out of his boots and this sends Boris into fits of laughter, and then Paul Heather can't help giggling and the skipper too. It does not seem so bad, standing in the freezing cold and gutting fish and their laughter rings out over the freezing waves.

Dworkin more smirks than laughs and although he heard the story and watched young Danny jump it does not really affect him. He puts down his cutting knife and smiles to show his blackened teeth to the others.

"Nature calls," he says to which the skipper nods. The Geordie man limps down the slippery deck through the fish and to the door that leads to the accommodation but he doesn't go through. He looks back over his shoulder to make sure no one is watching him. The skipper is busy with his fish, Danny and the others are facing the other way.

The Geordie moves past the door in the grey morning. He goes down to the orange lifeboat covered with a tarpaulin at the back of the ship. It is the boat the crew will use if the trawler gets into difficulties or sinks and it's not just a wooden rowboat; it has bunks below and is crammed with emergency food and flares, and anything they might need if they were adrift in the North Sea. Dworkin checks nobody is watching again before he gently taps on one of the portholes with his knuckle. Ra-ta-tat tat. There's movement behind the thick glass and rustling. Dworkin can't suppress a genuine grin across his face as he hears the panel sliding open and sees the two eyes of his accomplice. The big Scotsman peeps out at him through the tarp.

"Two days," whispers Dworkin. "The fish room will be full enough in two days. You ok in there?" He can see the flash of the man's white teeth.

"Aye. Nice and warm," whispers the stowaway.

CHAPTER TWELVE

The fish keep coming. They shoot the trawl almost as soon as it is hauled in. The skipper orders it up again after two hours then it's full once more. Here is the business end of trawling, hauling up, cutting, washing, and packing on ice. The skipper wants the fish room full before the first cod they have caught goes anywhere near rotten. Danny works like he has never done before. He works till his hands shake and his legs wobble. The skipper swaps them around and so sometimes Danny is down in the fish room with Paul Heather. Where before there was nothing in the big hold, now, the space is more than half full of fish, iced, and stacked on the aluminium trays.

As Danny walks to the accommodation and off shift, Sparky calls him over to the stern. Just before the lifeboat, there is a large and stinky metal vat where he pours another bucket full of cod livers. It's the wireless operator's job to make the oil that sells so well to the pharmacy company. It's profitable. The man recoils from the stink of the liquid as he steps from the vat and puts the liver bucket down.

"What is it?" asks Danny.

"I just wanted to have a word," he says as he takes out a cigarette. As an afterthought, Sparky offers one to the lad. Danny doesn't smoke but he is some two thousand miles away from home. Why shouldn't he have a cigarette? Sparky lights it up for him. Danny feels his head spin when he takes his first drag and coughs. It's vile. His eyes water. "The skipper's happy with you, Danny. You're a good worker. You'll do well out of this trip." The lad grins and his lungs spasm from the cigarette smoke.

"How long have we got left?"

"If we keep going like this, we'll be full in no time." Sparky takes another pull on his cigarette.

"I just want to give you a word of warning."

Danny is perplexed. "What for?" Sparky looks like he does not want to say what he is going to, but he feels like it's his duty to the deckie learner. Everyone has shown the lad something so far, now it's the wireless operator's turn.

"The crew are not your mates," he says. "I mean, they won't let you go overboard, but they're not your best friends. They'll take advantage if they can. Keep yourself to yourself. Do you know what I mean?"

"No," says Danny.

"These blokes are working men, the skipper too. If you work as hard as you can, they'll make you work harder. All I'm saying is that if you keep on like you have been for the next few days, you'll be fit for nowt. Look at Paul Heather, he works at a pace like his brother. Simo is more about cracking jokes than really cracking on. Boris takes it steady and have you seen how many times Dworkin has gone off for a toilet break. He ought to see a doctor."

"Why are you telling me this?" asks Danny. He has forgotten to take a toke on his cigarette and it's burning down to his fingers.

"I was like you are, once," says Sparky. "I was a nice lad who wanted to please. It took me a good few trips to realise that I was working twice as hard as anyone else and not getting the same amount of pay. Think about it." Danny examines what this wireless operator is telling him, and it makes sense.

"What about the skipper?"

"Nobody wants you to get hurt, lad, but the skipper is just the same. He'll have you take the strain while he does something else. He's a damn sight better than most other skippers, I'll give you that, but he's still here to catch fish, and if he messes this one up, the company will drop him."

"What about the bosun? What happened to him?"

"That's another thing," says Sparky. "I can't be sure he slipped and hit his head. That Paul Heather has a nasty eye as well and Dworkin is too quiet. There's a temper on Mike Heather and… I don't know. I don't know about the skipper either." Sparky realises from his cricketing days not everyone on the team is playing for the team. Most play for themselves. He doesn't want this young man to get taken advantage of too much, like he was.

"Just look after yourself, alright? Keep your head down, and we'll make it back to Hull. If we're lucky, there'll be a few quid in it."

"I will."

"Go see Vicky before you go to bed, get some food in you." Danny shrugs his shoulders. He's too exhausted to eat.

"I don't know if I can face any more fish and chips," says Danny.

"You never know," says Sparky. "It might be fish and mash." He watches the lanky boy stagger back to the accommodation.

Danny steps into the darkness of the bunk room and then sits down on the bed. His hands are swollen again, and his legs buzz with fatigue. Boris says that it can take five days for your hands to go back to normal after you've been gutting. He struggles with his boots and then takes off his socks to reveal puffy white feet before he lays back onto his bed and his eyes close. Another figure staggers into the bunk room, a little shorter than Danny and only a bit older; it's the Rat. He has also been gutting fish on deck which he resents. If they weren't men down then he wouldn't have to do so. He wants to take his anger out on someone.

"That's m-m-my bunk," says the Rat. The stutter does not lend itself to sounding cruel. Danny cannot even move his head. "I said that's m-m-my bunk." The apprentice engineer tries to sound as horrible as he can. It is not his bunk, no one has their own bunk. Danny ignores him because he is so exhausted. "Get out of m-m-my bunk," and the Rat leans down and pulls Danny's legs off the thin, foam mattress and from under the rough blanket. It's unnecessary, Danny half wakes.

"What's your problem?" he asks.

"You a-a-are." The Rat reaches down, grabs Danny by one of his shoulders and pulls him up from the bunk, so he falls on his elbows on the floor. Danny is used to being physically attacked but it does not mean that he feels comfortable with it, and as he lands on the hard floor and cracks his head, his mind fires in anger. What's he done to deserve this? Danny responds quickly by kicking at the Rat's legs and in the gloom, the apprentice engineer falls on him and pins him to the ground. The two struggle for a minute with Danny underneath. The few more years of experience and the heavy work down in the engine room make the Rat tougher than he is. He brings his ugly face down to look at Danny below him.

"You s-s-stay off my bunk," says the Rat as he puts his knees on Danny's shoulders and applies his whole weight. There is resentment in the young man's voice along with his hooked nose and slightly buck teeth. Danny is not using his bunk but the Rat needs an excuse to attack him, for since Danny is not yet experienced enough to work like a normal deckhand, the Rat believes the skipper has roped the apprentice engineer in to gut, which is below his position. Also, the Rat has always been at the bottom of the ladder in terms of strength, social status and pay and now there is someone lower than he. It is time to pass on the debts he has kept. He keeps his weight on Danny for every occasion Mike Heather has kicked him in the arse, or Greasy Joe has told him he's too stupid to learn, or the skipper has made him wash the deck after the fish are all gone. That's what this is really about. Power.

To Danny, struggling under the apprentice engineer, it just feels like pain. He grabs out at the side of him with his free hand and finds the floppy rubber of his boot, he pushes the Rat upwards and swings it. The heavy sole connects with his cheekbone and sends him reeling to the side of the bunkroom. Danny does not care about the power struggle. He does not ever want to set foot on a trawler again. He's angry. He struggles to his feet with the boot in his hand.

The light goes on.

Standing at the door is Mike Heather. He notes the boot in Danny's hand, the fallen position of the Rat and the red mark on his face where he's been hit. Mike reads what has happened immediately and can see Danny is about to give him a beating. Tension has to be defused with humour. It's what they do, so he cannot help himself from saying:

"What are you doing on the floor, Rat boy?" and then, "Is he bothering you, lad?" even though it's clear that Danny has the upper hand. Danny drops the boot and staggers back onto his bunk then lays down. The Rat gets himself up and brushes the wet fish goop from Danny's boot off his face; he looks wide-eyed at Mike Heather, and once more he is the lowest creature on the trawler, lower even than the deckie learner who he has tried to dominate so unsuccessfully. Mike Heather is changing his socks.

"You ladies ought to be getting some sleep. It's not a school trip to Scarborough, you know." His voice is deep and slow. The Rat crawls into his bunk and Mike Heather turns out the light behind the door as he leaves so the little bunk room is in darkness again with the white corridor light bleeding through the cracks. The apprentice engineer looks up into the night and feels small. He did not want to work on the ships, not at all, but his father had thought it would be the best thing for a feckless, angry little boy. The outbursts that the Rat had shown at home to his mother and sister on Dairycoates Lane were soon quelled on a trawler, replaced with fear. It had been easy for him to shout at a kind mother who never told him off and a weak sister who was afraid of him while his old man was away. He had been a tyrant on the stage at home and now, out here in the real world, he doesn't even have a bit part.

Danny turns over in his bunk. He gets a sense of the Rat now and the aggression he saw in the engine room when Greasy Joe gave him a tour. There was no need for any of that. Danny knows what a bully is, he has studied one close up for as many years as he can remember, and he knows how they work. As sleep takes over him, Danny realises how nice it has been on the trawler so far, how he has not been afraid of random attack either physical or verbal. He hasn't had to listen to one of his father's outbursts as he shouts, as loud as he can, about a fork that is not clean, or shoes that have not been put in the cupboard under the stairs. In a way, these rough seafaring men have shown him how ordinary people behave. Danny likes it. He wants to be an ordinary person too where you don't fight or shout or get angry about the slightest thing. It's only because he doesn't want any more trouble with the Rat that he says into the darkness:

"Touch me again and I'll break your nose." The Rat pulls his blanket up, over his head. Rather than make him feel scared and want to leave him alone, Danny's comment has fired him up.

He'll get that bastard in the end, he thinks.

The cycle goes around again. Wake. Eat fish. Stagger onto deck. Gut fish. Watch the winch pull the trawl out of the Barents Sea. Observe Simo pull the cod end open and see it spill onto the fish deck in a big, silver splash. Gut fish. Gut cod. Help Boris gut a giant halibut. Gut a bream. Examine something that looks like it came straight out of hell then throw it overboard. Fix the net. Get it ready. Shoot the trawl again. Gut fish. Go for a piss and feel your hands shake as you wonder if you still can. Watch the fish spill onto deck. Listen to Boris talk about what he's going to do after he never has to go trawling again. Eat fish, again. Listen to Mike Heather eat fish and slurp tea. See the nasty eyes of Paul Heather. Listen to American Services Radio piped through the cans onto the deck. Gut fish. Sleep and gut fish in your sleep. Feel the boat rock and roll beneath your feet. Taste sea water on your lips. Get seawater in your eyes. Get seawater down your wellies and in your underpants. Listen to Greasy Joe detail some of the girls he's done. Gut fish. See the eyes of the Rat looking at you as if you have murdered his mother. Shiver as you sit on the toilet. Gut fish. Don't change your clothes. Feel your hands raw even though they are in gloves all day. Smoke a fag that Sparky gives you even though you don't smoke. Listen to the wind rattling the cables on the trawl winch. Gut fish. Stand in the fish room and shovel ice onto the fish. Listen to Mike Heather eat. Eat fish. Feel cold. Wonder when you'll get home or if you want to go home or what home is.

Danny sometimes thinks this is how it must have been in the war, but Simo says he worked with lads who did fight in the war and they told him trawling was a lot worse. Then it's back to it. Sleep. Dream. Eat fish. Catch the Rat glaring at you. See Dworkin's googly eye, watch his daft, straight-legged limp. Listen to the gulls fighting in the ship's wake for the guts that they chuck overboard.

Just as Danny feels there is nothing human left of him, that his hands are not his own and he is looking through someone else's eyes; he sees the smiling face of Paul Heather come up from the fish room. This is strange because he does not smile. Danny watches from the deck as the man goes to the wheelhouse. He sees the grin on the skipper's face as he steps outside and grabs for the ship's brass bell by the rope clanger. He rings it and the noise seems foreign against the backdrop of screaming gulls and the wind. Simo is fixing the net to reshoot, his shoulders drop in relief.

"Thank God for that," says Boris.

"What is it?" asks Danny,

"We're full," says Dworkin, leaning on a railing with a fish in his hand. "It means we're going home."

Danny feels like crying.

They still have a deck full of fish to cut and pack away but that will be it. It will be easy. He grins at Boris who beams back. Big Mike Heather yells an American style yahoo into the morning air, and the skipper turns the wheel in front of him. Although he's been going in lots of different directions, he likes to give the boat a good swing round, right round, so the crew know they are going home and he knows he is going back too.

In the wheelhouse, the skipper breathes out. The fish room is full. All he has to do now is get home and that's it. Just sail back, get off the boat, collect his money the next day, find Boyce and then tell him he's never going to sea again. Then, walk down West Dock Ave and into Rayners, buy each one of these lads a pint, including Dworkin, and then go home back to his lass. That will be it. Never again. He will have done it and they can start fresh. The skipper sees his wife on the edge of the sofa. He can see her curly brown hair and her soft eyes looking at him and smiling when he tells her he will not ever be going back, despite the money. Though a life at sea is all the skipper has ever known, he has promised her. It is all so easy in the skipper's mind as he turns the wheel around and grins at Sparky. He thinks of the bosun's body in the fish room covered in ice. There will be an investigation. There will be paperwork to fill in and questions, and it will be Skipper Bird who will tell his thin misses from Gillett Street what has happened. He sighs, it's not something he has ever had to do before.

CHAPTER THIRTEEN

The feeling on the deck is good. Though they still have fish to get through, Paul Heather has opened the half bottle of whiskey he brought with him and is uncharacteristically offering it round. He takes a swig and then passes it to Boris, who he knows is not a drinker. The old man gives it to Danny because he knows the lad will not be able to take more than a sip. Danny goes to pass it to the Rat in a show of conciliation, but Paul Heather snatches it back.

"I'm not wasting it on him," he says, and there is a flash of resentment in the Rat's eyes. He has worked as hard as anyone these last few days. Mike Heather takes the bottle and empties a good deal of it down his throat before his brother gets it back and looks upset. The good feeling returns as they gut the last of the fish on board. Danny now feels the life of a trawlerman is not so hard after all. There are even moments such as these where he feels happy to be there, like he's part of the machine, one of the boys even.

"I'm off to see our lass when I get home," says Mike Heather. It's tenderness from the big man. He says whatever he thinks and he continues to work as he talks. "I might take her to the pictures. I might get her a new dress or a ring. She makes me laugh and I feel safe with her."

"Straight to Rayners for me," says Paul. "Back home, sit in the bath in the kitchen, drink two bottles of brown, stick on my suit and straight to Rayners. I hope we get in on a Thursday. Friday night, pissed, Saturday night Bailey's and then get back out to sea Sunday morning."

"I might leave my kitbag onboard," says Boris. "I won't be needing it again, will I?"

"I'm gonna go and see my dad," says Danny as he looks out across the ocean. His voice sounds final. He turns back to the lads. They have stopped working for a minute and are concentrating on this tall deckie learner with his hair longer than it should be. "I'll see my old boy. I'm gonna tell him he can't push me and my mam around anymore. I've had enough of it. I'm gonna sort him out." As soon as he has said this, he wishes he hadn't. It's not like he's thought about it. The idea just occurred to him now—that he would confront the man.

"You gonna sort him out, are you?" asks Paul. He can read the slight anger on the lad's voice.

"Something like that," says Danny. Paul can see he has hit a nerve with this and he wants to explore.

"Does he hit you?" Danny does not reply. "Does he hit your mam?" They continue gutting the fish and Danny regrets saying anything. He has been lulled into a false sense of security by the men. Sparky was right, he should have kept himself to himself, but Paul Heather likes this lad and he likes the fact he is going to sort his dad out.

This is what Paul would do.

"Do you remember when you sorted our dad out, Mike?" The big man stops gutting and wrinkles his nose at his brother. He looks back through time. Far from making a joke, Paul Heather, with a good glug full of Teacher's Scotch in his gullet wants to offer help.

"I do," says Mike.

"Our old man was a big bastard as well, lad," says Paul Heather. "He was bigger than Mike here and quicker than me. He was a vicious sod. He'd attack you when you were pissed or asleep and he was horrible to our mam, wasn't he, Mike?" The big man nods. "He was a boxer too, back in his day was our dad, semi-professional. He used to be second on the bill on when there was a big fight at The Bootherferry Club. He knew how to swing a punch so it hurt. Mike showed him though, didn't you, Mike?" There is a ring of admiration in Paul's tone as he looks up and across at his brother.

"I gave him the clothesline," Mike says with triumph. He

steps forward towards Danny and swings out his fist, slow and delicate with the knuckles turned inward, not in anger but only to demonstrate how his clothesline is performed. It's a big hook finishing with Mike's knuckles just behind Danny's ear. Mike taps him very lightly. "That's the spot that knocks you out, that's why you're not allowed to do it in a boxing ring. I did him with it in the kitchen and he went down like a sack of spuds." Paul Heather nods.

The clothesline.

Paul wants to add that after this, his old man never hit them again and never pushed his mother down the stairs, but this is not true. They fought with their father on many occasions subsequently, and although Paul would never say, it is the main reason why he knows how to hurt a man so well. The fighting did not actually stop until his father was in his early sixties, and Paul broke his jaw with one of those old-fashioned irons you used to put on the fire to get hot. The old man could never pronounce his words properly after that.

Danny wonders if the clothesline would work on his father.

"You gotta get in quick, mind," explains Mike. "Get that punch in first before they can do anything.' It is the same punch he used in The Silver Cod and in the fights in prison which got him extra months behind bars. He grins.

The Rat wonders if the clothesline would work on Danny.

At the first sitting for tea, there's only Sparky absent and in the wheelhouse. The rest of the lads sit in the galley waiting for Vicky to pass them down their food. It will be five days or so before they get back to dock and the safety of Hull. There will still be things to do, nets to mend and tools and rooms to clean down, but for the most part they're done. Vicky passes down white tin bowls of yellow soup.

"What's this?" calls Simo.

"It's fish chowder," says Vicky from behind the swing doors where he is collecting more bowls. He would one day like to go to the college in town and become a real chef who works in a bistro and knows French and has one of those tall hats. Mike Heather sniffs at the delicate soup, lifts the bowl to his lips and drinks the lot in two solid gulps. The rest of the trawlerman take a bit more time. They pass the dishes back in. Vicky gives out the same old, fried fish and mash with beans. Despite this, the feeling is still good.

"How much do you reckon we've got in there, skipper?" asks Simo.

"Not as much as I would have hoped," says Birdie. He has undone his shirt in the heat of the galley. This is a lie, of course. The fish room is full, but to boast so openly to the crew of his own ship would be unlucky. There are still many things that could go wrong even though all they have to do is sail home.

"I won't be coming back," says Boris. The men know this but do not believe it. They have all heard it a million times.

"You'll be bored in a week," says Simo. "Your misses will be sick of you and all you'll do is tell her stories about the sea."

"You're just jealous, Simo, you're jealous because this summer, I'll be sat in my chalet five minutes' walk from Hornsea beach, and you'll be here covered in fish guts and eating Vicky's French soup."

"There'll always be a spot for you here, Boris," says the skipper. "It won't be the same on the Cuckoo without you." There is sarcasm in the skipper's voice.

"What about you, lad?" he calls to Danny. "You coming back out with us?" The skipper knows he, Skipper Richard Bird, will not be coming back at all, but he does not want to tell this to the crew. Not yet.

"I dunno, skipper," answers Danny. "I dunno if my mam

will let me." There are smiles at this.

"How come she let you this time?" asks Mike Heather.

"I didn't tell her," he says. Danny has grown up a good deal right before their very eyes.

"I think it'll be five days before we get to port," says the skipper. "If the weather's bad, maybe a day more." He wants to tell the lads how well they have done and how hard they have worked, but this would be unlucky aboard a Hull Trawler. It would be boastful and arrogant; the skipper is neither of these things. He does not want to make her angry.

"I'm off on one of those freezer ships, I am." It's Mike Heather engaging his brain to mouth effectively. He refers to trawlers like The Nelson, which are brand spanking new. These ships don't just catch and gut fish, they fillet them as well. They are almost like floating factories with working hot showers and proper beds and food that is not fish every day. Mike thinks he may prefer this.

"Joe here will be off to see his girlfriends, isn't that right Joe?" says Paul Heather. The slightly flabby man looks instantly flustered. He has a habit of spending his money on that sort of lady and because he is embarrassed about it, they will make fun of him. Paul Heather has also visited these ladies but does not give a toss what anyone thinks.

"Mind your own business," answers Greasy Joe. The Rat sits next to him and wonders if anyone will ask him what he is planning to do, but he is invisible in his blue dungarees with his pointed nose and buck teeth. He might as well be a picture on the wall.

"What about you, Dworkin?" asks the skipper. "What have you got planned when you get home?" The sailor looks off past him and shows his rotten teeth in a half-grin.

"I dunno," he answers. The skipper allows him a minute to respond but the Geordie keeps looking towards the galley door. The skipper does not trust this, every sailor knows what he will do as soon as he gets back. Perhaps the man does not want to say. Even so, the skipper has not been much impressed with this Geordie fisherman with his gammy leg. He does not share stories like a normal trawlerman would, and it's like he's waiting for something. Maybe he's just waiting to get home. What does the skipper care now, anyway? They are on their way back, and the fish room is full. Apart from the dead bosun, this has been a good trip.

"Come on, Jim," says the skipper and the little dog hops up on his lap and sniffs at the empty plate on the table. Jim looks across at Dworkin, and his lips curl back in a low, threatening growl.

Dworkin grins back.

The Cuckoo falls heavily to one side. It's not just the ebb and flow of the waves. The skipper drops his knife and looks up. It's like they are banking to the left and too harshly at this speed. Way too harshly. The whole trawler tips unnaturally. It's the same feeling as they had on the River Tees. The skipper stands with a look of concern as Jim jumps down. He makes his way to the door of the galley, through the long corridor and up the steps outside to the deck above.

The door of the wheelhouse is wide open to the wind, and Sparky is laid on the floor as the boat continues to lurch to one side. The skipper goes for the wheel first to correct the spin. Paul Heather is behind him and kneels down to Sparky. The man has a bruise on the side of his head. As Paul turns him, a line of blood runs down his face. The wireless radio operator's eyes flicker. He's not dead.

"He's been clobbered round the head," says Paul. "This time it's bloody obvious." The skipper gets the ship back on course, and they feel the boat coming up straight once more. He crouches next to Sparky and looks at his pale face.

"It was that bloody Geordie," says Paul Heather.

"He was sat in the same room as us, you clot. Everyone was." Mike Heather appears at the wheelhouse door.

"Is he gonna be alright?" he asks.

"I dunno, he's breathing," says the skipper.

"Well if it wasn't that Dworkin and we were all in the galley. Who the hell's hit him?" Paul glares at the skipper like he ought to know because he's in charge.

"There must be someone else on board," says the skipper. "That's all it can be unless he fell like the bosun did." Mike Heather points to the VHF radio where Sparky usually sits; there is a big dent in the metal and between the dials where it looks like something has hit the equipment. All the wires at the back have been ripped out as well.

"That's the radio gone," he says. The skipper helps Paul to sit Sparky up in the leather chair at the back of the wheelhouse. They lean his head against the wall under a rolled-up jacket and he groans. The skipper turns to Mike.

"I want everyone up here, everyone, including Greasy Joe and the Rat and Vicky too. We've got a stowaway."

CHAPTER FOURTEEN

The whole of the crew is assembled in the little wheelhouse that looks down on the bow of the ship. The seas are a bit rough but nobody notices this. Not even Danny. The faces are serious though they should not be with a full fish room.

"A stowaway. Are we in Treasure Island?" asks Simo. "I thought it was an Agatha Christie film."

"How else could you explain it?" asks the skipper as he points to Sparky with a bruise swelling on his temple. The blonde man has not yet regained his senses. Perhaps he never will.

"There's no one on this ship apart from us," says Boris. "We crawl all over it every day. It's something else, I tell you." The skipper regrets now that he asked the crew here. It allows Boris to scare everyone again. "It's something unnatural, I tell you. It's the bosun. We shouldn't be carrying a dead body; it isn't right. That's what sunk the Thornella in 1953—they were carrying dead men." The skipper does not know the story, nor does he want to. It won't help them with the situation at all. "This is a bad trip, there are too many bad things that have happened," continues Boris again. "Better that we get the bosun's body out and drop it in the sea." The skipper looks at his crew crammed in the wheelhouse. Paul Heather's face wears a snarl and his brother has worried, flared nostrils behind him. Danny has a woolly hat pulled down over his hair and a permanent look of horror. The Rat considers his boots and his palms are sweaty. Greasy Joe is white with fear. Boris is terrified. There's only Simo who will not take it seriously, like he's been taught to.

There have been stowaways before on trawlers. When he was a deckhand, the skipper recalls wives who were smuggled on board and even other types of ladies. He's heard of little lads hiding away to follow their dads to sea, but they always get found within the first few days or as soon as they were hungry or needed to have a poo.

"Is the radio totally dead?" asks Danny. It's a much better question than worrying about ghosts.

"It's had it," answers the skipper. "Whoever wrecked it, knew what they were doing. Now, this is how we're going to get along. There's someone else on this trawler, and by the looks of it, they mean to do us some harm. I want two men together at all times. Grab something you can use if you have to," the skipper nods at Vicky. He is already carrying his 40-ounce rolling pin which he chose in favour of a chopping knife.

"This is how it works. Simo and Vicky, I want you two below deck, search the quarters, even my room. Search the cupboards and the shower, the mess and everywhere in the kitchen no matter how small. That means all the cupboards and under all the units." The skipper is confident Vicky can handle himself, he's not naturally aggressive, but the rolling pin will swing if he gets spooked. He can trust Simo to do the right thing.

"Mike and Paul will check the deck and the fish room. Check that bosun's body as well, just to be sure."

"Why do we have to do that?" says Paul with indignation.

"Just do it," whispers the skipper. "Boris and Dworkin, you lads check the stern. Look in the lifeboat, check the liver tanks, check every barrel we've got on deck as well. Rat, take the lad here and check over the engine room. I know you and Joe spend your life in it, but that doesn't mean there isn't someone there. Joe, you nip out onto deck and grab one of those crocodile toothed spanners and bring it back, you and me will stay here. Got it?"

"If there's anyone on board, skipper, they'll have a very hard time, you do realise that?" It's the snide face of Paul Heather in a whisper almost. It's not a question. The skipper licks his lips. The man will have a free reign to do what he wants if he does encounter anyone.

"It's still murder, even if it's in the middle of the North Sea, so if you find someone, you can rough them up, that's all."

"There's nobody on board, skipper." Boris has taken his cap off to reveal his thick white hair. His eyes are wide and red. "I knew this was my last trip," he says, "and I knew I'd die at sea. Mrs Moore, from Liverpool Street read my mother's tea leaves when I was a little lad. She said one of us boys would die at sea. Our Jason and Jonny, they're both in their seventies now and so it's just me left. I knew. I said to our LeeAnn this would be my last trip. Whatever it is, has come to take me away." His face is stricken with fear and terror. Mike Heather leans forward and slaps the old man across his face, there is no real force in the blow, but it staggers Boris and shocks him like a cold shower. He stops and looks up at the faces around him. Perhaps it is true that he will die at sea, maybe Mrs Moore from Liverpool Street was correct when she frightened Boris's young mother back in 1924. Either way, he cannot escape it. There is no need to be afraid. Perhaps there really is something evil that treads the deck of the Cuckoo in the frozen winter dusk. Whatever the truth is, there is no need to give it a name. Give your fear a value then it's real, and it can hurt you. Boris realises his demons have got the better of him.

"I'm sorry, lads," he says. Mike Heather squeezes his shoulder in friendship.

Like the skipper asked, Greasy Joe grabs a heavy crocodile toothed spanner from one of the tool bags on the deck and brings it to the wheelhouse. Mike Heather takes out his gutting knife. Danny follows the Rat down to the engine room while Vicky and Simo make their way to the quarters and the galley. Boris takes the lead as he and Dworkin go to the stern of the trawler to check the lifeboat.

In the wheelhouse, Greasy Joe leans against the back wall

with the spanner in his hand. His fat hands are clammy with sweat and he wipes his brow with his handkerchief.

"Do you think there is anyone on board, skipper?" he asks. The two have sailed together for a long time. There's a good sense of no-nonsense between them.

"There better be. I'm not sailing a ghost ship," he turns to look at the engineer and, for the first time, Joe can hear what passes for fear in Skipper Bird's calm voice.

The Rat lifts the hatch to the engine room and keeps it open while Danny goes down before him. There's a red pilot light on down there which gives the pipes and the yellow engine a sci-fi feel. Danny's boots thud down the metal stairs to the bottom while the Rat closes the entrance behind.

The apprentice engineer follows and switches on the light about halfway down. It illuminates the engine room with a flicker as the neon bulb on the far wall comes to life. Danny walks over to the big engine and looks down both sides. The Rat picks up a spanner in his bony hand. There's an uneasiness to the noise of the engine that powers the swirling propeller in the cold sea outside. The tension between these two young men hangs in the warm air. Danny turns to him, he does not want to argue, and he wishes they had not fought the night previous.

"Look, I'm sorry about whacking you with that boot," he says, even though he was attacked first. The Rat has his head down as he considers the spanner in his hand. "I wasn't in your bunk, was I?"

"No," comes the answer. "I just w-w-wanted to get my own back." Danny looks confused.

"I haven't done owt to you." It's true. Danny has barely spoken to him.

"B-b-but you're just l-l-like them." This is the chain of abuse that runs in factories or families, dog packs or chicken coops—or this is the way it looks to the Rat.

"What's your name?" asks Danny.

"Steven," answers the lad. It is the first time on board the trawler that he has ever spoken his name, and both of them at once realise that it is unlucky to have said it. It's unlucky to call things by their real names on a trawler.

"I just want to get home, mate," says Danny. "I don't want any trouble." This might seem the most reasonable thing to say in such a situation, but to the Rat, it is just a display of weakness. If Danny had shown aggression, then the apprentice engineer might have backed off but as it is, he sneers at the deckie learner along his hooked nose. The Rat won't take Danny on face-to-face; he's tried that already. It will have to be something else.

"You c-c-check the right side and, I'll…," the Rat struggles with his sounds as he is caught on one of his big stutters, the words are trapped in his lips.

"Do you want me to check the left?" asks Danny. He nods. The noise from the engine is a constant banging. It would be an excellent place to hide. It's warm and safe, and yet, Greasy Joe would be here all the time with his apprentice. There would be nowhere for a stowaway to go. The two lads meet up at the other side of the engine, and big pipes stretch off into the darkness. The Rat nods his head and Danny checks around and under one of them. He half expects to see white eyes peeping out from below, but there is nothing there as he leans his head right under.

Danny gets a bad feeling from the Rat, like he might swing that spanner down on him at any minute. They look under the metal cupboard. The Rat can't help but check the four gauges above each piston and that they are all generating the same, smooth power to the engine. Danny noses around at the telegraph wheel where Greasy Joe receives his orders from the skipper above. It's a round dial with words on the bottom, fast, slow and half. Running the engine is not an easy job, the Rat and Joe are both worth the money.

The two lads move along the small space between the engine where it is loudest. There is a row of tall, deep lockers at the side of the wall and Danny walks forward to them. He glances back to the Rat to make sure he's still following. The locker would easily be big enough for a man to hide inside. Both the lads realise this, suddenly, and stop.

Danny stands at the locker door and nods back at the apprentice. He puts his hand on the shiny catch of the locker as if to open it, and the Rat weighs the spanner to signal he will bash anyone who is inside. In the heat and the noise, it's the best they can do to communicate.

Danny's mouth is dry as he pulls open the locker door. There is nothing but darkness inside. He feels a sense of relief and looks over his shoulder to see a flash of movement.

The Rat swings the spanner at his head.

Danny ducks as it clips him on the shoulder, and he has no choice but to fall forward into the metal of the locker, headfirst and dazed. The Rat steps nearer, shoves him inside and closes one, then the other locker door behind. As Danny comes to his senses, he can hear something being fitted through the metal handles on the outside and locking him in. He bangs on the steel and it makes a clanging noise that is drowned out by the engine.

He's trapped.

The Rat gives himself a congratulatory smile and a little nod. He will have the last laugh.

Boris has picked up a deck club, they are the tools trawlermen use to clobber big halibut if they flap around too much. It's like a truncheon, and he carries it low by his side. It would do a man some considerable damage. Boris is nervous. He is more nervous about the tea leaf prophesy than anything else. It plays on his mind like it has since he first heard it many years ago. As they head down past middeck, the floodlights illuminate the front of the trawler, and it makes the dusk of the stern where they are, much gloomier. Boris checks over his shoulder to see Dworkin following him.

"They'll be nobody else on board," says Boris. "You'll see. How could someone hide on a ship like this? There's barely enough room for twelve men."

"They could have crawled on somehow," says the Geordie from behind. "There are some clever fellas out there. They could have crawled on in the dead of night before you even set sail." It sounds like there is the ring of admiration in Dworkin's voice.

"Aye, but they'd have to be mermaids to do that. I've never heard of mermaids in the North Sea. It's too cold for anyone, let alone pretty girls." In the Ferens Art Gallery back in Hull City centre, opposite the toilets that have a statue of Queen Victoria built on them. There is a painting entitled 'Ulysses and the Sirens'. A muscular figure of Ulysses is strapped to the mast of a rowing boat while semi-naked, svelte mermaids crawl up the side singing. It's tastefully done, but the image has left a powerful impression, even forty years later on Boris. In his bunk of a night, he sometimes dreams he is in that scene, and the mermaids with their porcelain skin and smooth hands are taking him away to the bottom of the warm sea. It briefly removes him from the dread he is in right now, as he thinks of it.

"They could have hidden on the lifeboat?" says the Geordie. Boris stops and looks back again. He wrinkles his brow.

"Aye, they could have done, but it would have been cold in there, terribly cold. You'd have to be some sort of monster to keep warm in all this." They go past the stink of the cod liver oil tanks and then to the stern proper. There's just enough light to see the wake in the water behind them. Boris notices the tarpaulin usually tied fast around the top of the lifeboat is undone and pulled back. The old man does not put two and two together, neither the words of Dworkin, nor this tarp that has been tampered with. Boris's mind won't deal with reality as quickly as it does superstition or dreams or what might be, rather than what is.

"Some daft bastard has been pulling on the lifeboat," he says in disbelief. His fingers go to the rope that holds it in place to fix it back up. As he does so, he sees a very tall, hulking figure a few feet in front of him. It's a shape he does not recognise and the square jaw silhouetted against the dusk sky is not familiar. He breathes in sharply as he steps back and feels Dworkin's knife pressed against the small of his back.

"This here is the Bull," whispers Dworkin in the softest voice Boris has ever heard him use. "Shout or make a move, and I'll cut your throat like you're one of them codfish." Boris feels his stomach drop in fear. "We're taking over this trawler, old man."

Those tea leaves might have been right after all.

CHAPTER FIFTEEN

There's no point in banging.

The noise of the engine is so loud, Danny does not expect that anyone can hear him if he shouts or bangs. He has tried pushing at the door, but there's some sort of implement through the handles on the outside that stops them opening. Danny is philosophical about the whole episode. At least he is warm, at least his feet are dry, and he has somewhere to lean. He might as well take the opportunity to rest, it won't be his fault he's slacking off. In fact, the Rat may have done him a favour.

For a good ten minutes, Danny waits, half-sleeping as the trawler around him rocks on the waves and the noise of the engine clangs and hums outside the locked cabinet. He dreams of home and Johno. He thinks about school and the hustle and bustle of Hessle Road and how far away it seems to him now. It's as if he lived a different life in those days, almost like he was another person.

He thinks about his dad as well. The old man will be volcanically angry, so totally red hot with rage that Danny may be throttled on the kitchen table. Far from being worried by this as he may have been weeks previous, Danny considers the problem differently. Like a cat backing off into a corner against a vicious dog, there may be another way to deal with his father. What about Mike Heather's clothesline? That's what Paul told him to do. Perhaps Danny does not need to stand for the beatings anymore. Perhaps, after he has been washed overboard and back on, found his sea legs and has become a man; perhaps he can put his father on his arse and then he and his mam can go about their lives as ordinary people. Danny could live his life like he does on the trawler with regular folk who don't get angry and swing their fists, apart from the Rat. Danny feels the steel of determination run through him, it's a power that simmers with anger. When he gets back to Hessle Road and then Woodcock Street, he'll give his dad something to think about in the form of Mike Heather's clothesline to the back of the head. He'll watch the bastard crash back into the kitchen table. Danny feels hatred coarse through him. It runs through his legs and bares his teeth, makes his heart beat and his eyes burn with revenge. It reminds him of someone he knows only too well. He sighs, and feels the anger leave his body.

It reminds him of his father.

He rests his face on the smooth inside of the locker door then tries to push it open again. The spanner through the handles rattles outside. Danny thinks about the crew, his friendship with big Mike Heather, Sparky's advice next to the stink of the cod liver oil vat, how he has learned to gut fish and work like a man. These are things he can take with him, things he can use in the real world. He hears the advice of the skipper in his ears, if he needs any help then he should go and see him. When they find out Danny is not there, they will worry, perhaps the Rat will not say anything and they will worry more.

Danny remembers there may be someone else on board who has cracked Sparky round the head, so he should make more of an effort to get out. He rattles at the door handles again and they do not budge. Peering through the gap to the engine room outside, Danny can see the steps up to the hatch and the accommodation over the big yellow engine that thumps and clangs. He can see the telegraph wheel as well if he moves to the side. They'll be looking for him and anyway, the engineer will be down here soon enough. Who else is going to look after it? Who else is going to pull the handle on the wheel and control the speed?

Danny waits another five minutes before he sees the hatch at the top of the stairs open. He sees the boots of Greasy Joe and his blue dungarees as he walks down. Danny smiles. The engineer will let him out. There are other feet behind the fat man. They are big and solid army boots with thick black socks under army camouflage trousers. Danny wonders who would wear those.

Joe comes into full view at the bottom of the stairs. His fat cheeks are red and his glasses are at an angle like he's been in a fight. As he moves off, Danny can see why he looks that way. Behind him is a much larger man, bigger even than Mike Heather with a black jacket, a beanie hat, and a close-cropped ginger beard. He has small eyes and a square-jaw with a cold expression. Danny feels fear as he steps back against the wall of the metal locker. His chest tightens.

Who is he? Danny squints through the gap again. He cannot hear what the man is saying because of the engine, but he can see Joe is scared as he grabs the handle of the telegraph wheel and pulls it to slow and then round to half. Danny feels the engine hum in front of him as the power decreases. The trawler is turning. He can feel the movement around him. This ginger thug walks towards Danny and the locker he is trapped in. For a minute, the lad feels like he is going to walk right towards him, but the big man only checks the gauges on the cylinders to make sure they are working well and producing the same amount of power. He looks like he has sea legs also, because of the way he moves as the ship rocks on the waves.

Danny's mind races. They must be days away from land. Where can this man have come from? What's he done to Greasy Joe's face? Why is the ship turning?

The big ginger man has now returned to Greasy Joe and looks down on him. He waggles one of his fingers in threat. Then, as if the round shoulders of Joe are not scared enough, he grabs him by the throat and leans his face close as he gives harsh orders. Joe is wide-eyed in terror through his thick glasses. The man lets him go and begins back up the steps as the engineer's hand goes to his neck in pain. All the time the engine bangs and thumps. Danny watches him go up, open the hatch, and climb onto the deck above.

He thinks for a moment. There's still no point in banging, Joe still will not hear him at that distance even if he kicks the doors, even with the engine on a lower speed as it is. Perhaps he does not want to be freed either, maybe he is in the best place with a man like that about, and he should wait where he is until they get wherever they are going. His mouth is dry. Where's the Rat?

Greasy Joe composes himself and wipes his face down with a handkerchief from the back pocket of his dungarees. He coughs and then checks the gauges and dials at the far end of the room. He comes back along to the engine itself to check the diesel flow into the pistons. He flicks the dial of the first two, and when he checks the last, Danny bangs on the door of the locker and kicks it at the same time as hard as he can. Greasy Joe registers the noise and looks round in fear. He sees the spanner through the handles of the door, walks over as he wipes his hands and then removes it.

The locker swings open and Danny is inside. The engineer looks shocked to see him there and steps back.

"We thought they'd put you overboard," he has to yell to be heard.

"What's happened?" Joe looks back at the hatch above the stairs in fear and then back to Danny. The flabby man begins in earnest at a shout.

"We're being robbed, lad. It's Dworkin and that big Scott. He calls himself the Bull." He can hardly believe what he is saying as he looks into Danny's eyes in the darkness of the locker. "They're taking the boat."

"What?" asks Danny.

"They're taking the boat and the fish. The Geordie had that big bastard stashed away in the lifeboat."

"Like pirates?"

"Aye." There's movement from the hatch above the stairs, and as quick as he opened the locker doors, Greasy Joe shoves Danny back in, and shuts them again. Feet come down the stairs. This time it is Dworkin. Danny tugs the doors closed using the inside lip and watches the Geordie as he walks down the steps.

He looks different. Danny realises this version of Dworkin does not have a limp. He even moves with a spring in his stride, not at all like the shuffling, pathetic figure Danny worked next to.

Greasy Joe walks back to the telegraph wheel where Dworkin approaches and seems to ask him something. Joe replies, and without warning, Dworkin swiftly clips the engineer round the top of his head. It's a bit like watching Mike Heather clip the Rat. The Geordie follows up by saying something nasty and then turns to go back up the stairs. Danny tries not to breathe as he leans back against the wall of the locker where he has now been for more than an hour.

"Pirates," he whispers to himself.

When he is sure Dworkin and the big Scott have gone, Greasy Joe lets Danny out of the metal locker and sits him down behind the big bilge pipe that is painted black. If either of the two men do come back into the engine room, Danny can quickly scurry behind it. Joe has a cup of leftover tea that is cold. He has a sip and passes it to Danny. The lad takes a good glug, and it makes him feel better.

"They've locked the skipper in his quarters with Jim. The dog's going mad. They put the Rat in the fish room. I hope that kid is alright. He hates the cold. The bastards." Danny passes the cup back.

"What about Mike and Paul?"

"The big Scott and Mike went at it and he knocked our Mike clean out on the floor. They put them in the bunk room with Simo and Boris. They've got Paul up on deck and tied his hands behind his back with cable. They want him to freeze to death. It's been horrible." The engineer slugs back the rest of his cold tea. "They're making Vicky cook, and I'm down here with the engines. They've turned the boat off course. They say we're all going to Scotland, the boat and the catch."

"What are we gonna do?"

"You what?" says Joe. Even though he is worried and afraid, he is still deaf. Danny repeats himself, and the heavy man shakes his head. "I dunno. Do what they say? What else can we do?"

"Let Mike and Paul Heather at them."

"I told you, that big one slapped Mike around the deck like he was a ten-year-old kid. He's been battered. Paul's not big enough to take him on. I'm not young enough anymore neither. Nor is the skipper. Horrible big Scott, he is." Greasy Joe feels his neck where the Bull grabbed him, where the big fingers pushed at his soft throat.

"How did he get on board?"

"He's been in the lifeboat since Hull with the tarp over him, and as much tinned salmon as you could eat. He slipped out when nobody was looking to stretch his legs. That Dworkin, he's not lame at all. He just wanted to get out of work, and that's why the Scott laid in the life raft. He was waiting till you lads got a full fish room." Through gritted teeth, Greasy Joe speaks harshly of them. "They're gonna sell the fish and the trawler too."

"Do they know about me?"

"They think you've gone overboard; the Rat couldn't tell em what happened. It's a good job that lad can't say a thing when he's scared." Danny looks down at his boots and sighs. This is all a terrible upheaval for Joe who has been aboard the Cuckoo for many a year, but for Danny, who has been through the steepest of learning curves and who is terrified continuously, it is just a compounding of the fear. He's almost used to it.

"What about the bosun? Did they do him in?" Greasy Joe

looks down at Danny, and his skin is pale, his eyes are red through his thick-rimmed glasses.

"I think they did, lad." It has become more serious. "I think he must have." Danny stands up.

"What are you doing?"

"I'm going up on deck."

"No, you're not," says Greasy Joe. "You go up there, you'll get yourself killed, son. You'll stay down here with me, I'll nick you some food." Joe is sure of what he says. He's a man who knows about pumps and pipes and machines, he can calculate pressure and volume, has an understanding of electronics and physics, he is sensible. He knows when he has to dip his head in the face of a more powerful force. Danny is not so sure. He does not know what kind of a man he is, yet. If he is a brave one or a coward, if he is strong, if he's a leader or if he is just one of those people who have small parts to play in the story. Danny knows he can't hide here while the rest of the lads are in trouble upstairs. He's not a hothead like Mike Heather or as angry as Paul. He's not got the sarcasm of Simo, he's not as sneaky as the Rat or as worried about the future as Boris. He's not as intelligent as Sparky or as anal as the bosun was. Danny thinks about the skipper somewhere above and locked in his quarters like Greasy Joe told him. He thinks about the man with black hair and kind grey-blue eyes, someone who took him on board and showed him respect; respect that nobody else has ever given him. Not his mam or his dad or the teachers at school or the man at the boxing club he once went to, or the scout group he visited once or twice. Nobody in Danny's life has ever been there for him. It has been a lonely business, lonelier still now he knows what friendship and comradery is. Skipper Bird is who Danny aspires to be, the man who they all look to, the one who will not let you down.

Danny will not let him down.

CHAPTER SIXTEEN

Danny opens the hatch just a crack and peeps through into the darkness of the corridor. The pilot light is on at the end near the steps up to the deck outside. From the skipper's cabin, he can hear Jim barking behind the closed door. It looks empty, and so Danny goes up, closes the hatch gently behind him and then gets flat against the wall. In the outhouse at home, he and his father have a big collection of war comics. When it's warm enough, he sits on the lav and reads them, sometimes a whole one in a sitting so that he gets pins and needles in his arse cheeks. Danny knows he must be as stealthy as that World War Two officer creeping up on the German scout outpost in the darkness. He blinks and rubs his nose which he wants to blow. Danny is not naturally built to be quiet; he is gangly and a bit clumsy, his feet are too big and get in the way of him. He takes a deep breath; he has to be quiet. The dog barking is a good cover.

He creeps over to the skipper's cabin door and without a noise, he tries the handle. It's locked. He hopes the skipper has not seen it move from inside. The worst thing that could happen would be for him to shout out. Little Jim keeps on yapping behind the door in a steady unnerving bark. Danny is about to move along the corridor to the bunkroom when he hears the voice of the loud Scott getting closer.

"I'm gonna check that engine room again," he shouts. His accent is harsh, not the passionate lilt of the highlands but something crueller and more aggressive. Danny freezes there, standing in the corridor. Like this, he will be easy to see, even in the gloom. He nervously tries the handle of the storeroom door, this is where the skipper brought him on the first day. It's locked. His heart sinks. He tries it again with a bit more force and it turns. The storeroom is entirely black as he opens the door, steps inside and closes it again softly. A second later, the heavy Scott stamps down the corridor in his big army boots and opens the hatch to the engine room. Danny can hear him yelling at the engineer down there about something.

In the storeroom, the lad's eyes adjust to the darkness. Silently, he begins to feel around for anything he can use. There's a mop stood in a tin bucket in the corner and rows of oilskin jackets hanging and stinking along the wall. Danny checks the pockets for anything useful. There's a pouch of tobacco, some screws, a length of string and a bottle cap. In the last one, he finds a gutting knife with a broken handle. He slips this in the front pocket of his dungarees, you couldn't use it without cutting yourself. He crouches to check around on the floor, and his hands come upon a large metal box, he finds the catch in the darkness and opens it. Inside, Danny can feel fat cylindrical objects, and in the corner, his fingers run across the cold metal of a flare pistol. He breathes deeply as he picks it up. Danny has read about flare pistols in his war comics. He knows you load one of the heavy flares into the front then hold it above your head to shoot. Danny wonders what a flare would do to a man if it hit him.

There's the rumble of boots as the Scott comes up from the engine room and stomps past Danny behind the door. It runs through his mind to just open up and shoot the big man in his back, but there are many variables he has to take into account. He does not know how to load or shoot the flare gun without seeing it in the light. What if the flare does not kill him or even injure him? Then surely, the big animal will tear Danny's arms off or something equally horrible. He waits and listens to the man clumping around on the deck above. Where's Dworkin? What is Danny going to do? If he does not get this right first time, then he might be dead.

Jim is still barking. Danny opens the door to the storeroom and creeps out into the corridor once more. At the bunkroom, he tries the handle. It's locked. He whispers through the wall:

"It's Danny, is anyone there?" There's a scraping noise from inside, his voice will not be heard through the thick steel wall. "Can anyone hear me?" he whispers again. A pause. "I've got a flare gun."

There's no response from inside.

It is an impossible situation. A reversal of roles. Now, a man as big and powerful as Mike Heather needs Danny to rescue him. All the luck Boris has lies with him too. He holds even the skipper's fate in his hands and there will be none of them to guide him. Danny will have to do this alone, whatever that is.

The dog is still barking, and up on the deck, there is shouting. It's Paul Heather, yelling in a loud and aggressive voice in the darkness against the wind. Danny continues on into the shadows and down the corridor to the ladder that leads up onto the deck. The flare gun is in his right hand, and his legs are shaking. The boat rocks to one side, and he grabs hold of the railing as he looks to the floodlights above. He clambers up in silence and then out, into the cold night and wind of the North Water. He moves behind the rolled net and squats down in the darkness, not knowing what he's going to do. The swearing from the deck has stopped, and the only sounds are the wind and the clanging of the warp cable on the winch.

Below in the accommodation, Mike Heather has come round from the hammering blows the Scotsman delivered to him. It's taken him a while to unpick what happened. It was the speed and skill of a man trained to fight that bested him, it was no pub brawl where he could use his great strength and aggression to overpower the other. The Scott knew how to stop him, easily. He stands. He wants to fight the man again, and the only thing stopping him is that locked door. Boris looks up at him from one of the bunks with his tired and fearful eyes. Mike steps back in the bunkroom and lands the flat of his heavy boot on the iron in a thudding kick. The metal clangs. He knows this will take a long time and that it may not be successful so he pauses between each powerful kick.

"What's the point, son?" asks Boris.

"There's no point," answers Mike. His face is a grimace. He lands another kick on the iron, steps back and lands another. The noise is a constant thud. On deck above, Danny waits with the flare gun rattling in his hands as he shivers with cold. Mike Heather's banging gets attention. A much more agile Dworkin appears and walks past Danny crouching. He goes to where the noise is coming from and does not notice the lad as he climbs down the ladder.

"You'll just tire yourself out, man," he shouts to Mike. "You're not gonna get through that door." Mike carries on. "You'll need all the strength you can get when I chuck you overboard. The other ship's on its way now. There'll be more lads. We'll open that door and give you a proper beating as well. I'll give you a real taste of Tyneside. The more you keep banging, the worse it will be." Mike does not stop, nor does he respond. Dworkin sighs to himself in the darkness outside the locked iron door. "Hull," he scoffs in disgust.

When the Geordie returns to the deck, Danny has moved round and now squats just behind the trawl winch out of sight. In front of him is the body of Paul Heather. He's slumped to one side, but on his knees, and his hands are tied behind his back. Up in the wheelhouse, Danny can only just make out the big Scott through one of the little windows. At this angle he will not be able to see the lad. The wind is cold and Danny is not wearing his coat over his dungarees and jumper. His stomach growls in worry. He heard Dworkin say there was another boat coming so, whatever he is going to do, he will have to do it quickly. If others come, he may not have the chance to do anything at all. He takes a deep breath and peers out past the winch.

In the floodlights, Dworkin comes back to the body of Paul Heather. He picks the man up by his shoulders and returns him to an upright position on his knees. There's a bruise across Paul's cheek where he's been struck. Dworkin grins down on him.

"You had your bit of fun at my expense, but who's laughing now? Eh?" Paul Heather does not respond. Dworkin slaps him round the face so his body crashes into the deck. He bends down and then picks him up again. "I can go on like this all night, me." Dworkin sounds upbeat about the business. Paul Heather has not made a sound. Perhaps he's already dead. Fear tingles in Danny's legs. It's now or never. The boat pitches. The wind spray stings his ears. He needs to pee. His legs shake with cold and fear.

Get a grip, Danny boy.

He stands up, steps out into the light and levels the flare gun at Dworkin in full view of him. The man raises his eyebrows and grins, not so much in shock, more mild surprise. The Geordie holds up his hands slowly like he's not that worried.

"Get back, you bastard," says Danny. This makes Dworkin's grin bigger as he steps away.

"I was wondering where you'd got to. I thought you'd gone overboard." Even Dworkin's voice sounds more alert, and he looks younger than previous. Danny's arm shivers as he holds the flare gun; it feels heavy in his hands suddenly. "What are you gonna do with that?" asks Dworkin. Paul Heather whispers from beside him:

"Shoot him, lad." Paul's mouth is bleeding along with the bruise. Dworkin senses Danny's distress, he can see that this lanky lad with his woolly jumper on back to front over his dungarees, is not a fighter. The boy is too young to do anything nasty, too well brought up, too scared. The Geordie steps forward.

"You can shoot me, but you'll never get past the Bull.

He's gonna pull your head off." Dworkin's voice is playful.

"Shoot him, lad," whispers Paul Heather again. Dworkin steps forward and his hands come down to his hips. His expression changes to one of anger as he moves towards Danny. He's faced a lot worse than a flare gun held by some wet, Yorkie kid.

Danny raises the flare gun higher to Dworkin's face and squeezes the trigger. There's a click, and Danny half expects the nose of the pistol to explode into light, but there is nothing. Nothing at all but the wind and the fog and the rocking of the ship on the cold North Water. The Geordie's face switches from surprise to relief, and his smile returns.

"It's a bloody dud, you tit," he says.

This is the opening Paul Heather needs.

He has waited and planned for such a distraction and has saved up all his energy for it. He rocks forward, gets to his feet and rushes, headlong at Dworkin, crashing into the man's side and knocking him back. The Geordie is shocked as he lands against the bulkhead wall with a boom. Facing him, with his arms tied behind his back is the bloodied grimace of Paul Heather.

Paul has been in lots of fights. Lots of them. And not just against his dad or his brother, but men who wielded broken bottles or motorcycle chains. He has battled in the full moonlight of summer fields and winter city streets, from Chiltern Primary playground to the car park of Criterion, Paul has taken all comers, as a gang or alone against a gang. He has lost many and won some. It is all the same in the end win or lose, you will get hurt; it's just who gets hurt the worst. He does not feel angry at Dworkin only calm hatred. Paul has three weapons at his disposal, his two feet and his head—more than enough. Dworkin comes back at him and swings wildly, but rather than try to get out of the way, Paul Heather rushes forward, crashes into the Geordie and bites at his neck. It's a bold move. Paul has done this before.

There's no point in going at it halfway.

Like his dad used to say, there are no rules in a street fight, no moves that are off-limit and so long as you don't die, then you can do anything you want, and; it doesn't matter how much it hurts you, as long as it hurts the other fella more. Dworkin has been in fights as well, but never really on his own. Up and down the Bigg Market back in Newcastle, they fought in gangs so he's never really had to defend himself. Paul hurts him and he can feel the Hull trawlerman's teeth digging into his throat. His hands instinctively go towards Paul's head and face to try to push him off. As the Geordie staggers, Paul rips his face away and bites as hard as he can at the same time. Bits of Dworkin's unshaven stubble are in his mouth as he does so, along with the iron taste of blood. There's no time to pause. He draws his head back only slightly before he headbutts Dworkin, then draws back and butts him again, so the man's skull smacks on the bulkhead. He headbutts him over and over and feels something pop and crack in Dworkin's face, but he does not stop. Paul Heather knows that this is his only chance, he cannot allow Dworkin to recover at all, even if this means damaging himself beyond reason.

Danny's heart races in fear as he watches Paul Heather stagger back. He looks him up and down, and his face is splattered with gore, it could be his own or Dworkin's. He grins. Dworkin's body slides down the bulkhead with his head at an angle, motionless.

"You're a star, lad," he whispers.

"There's another boat coming," says Danny, breathless. "We have to get the Scottish fella." Paul shakes his head.

"Not me, lad." Danny can see the light dimming in Paul Heather's eyes. He's beyond exhausted as he sinks to his knees. "Put the flare in the gun the right way round," he says. Danny nods. "Go for his legs." With that, Paul drops to his knees and falls forward. His face rests against the deck.

The fog seems thicker.

It drifts out of the sea and wraps around Danny as he stands, shivering in his roll-neck jumper over his dungarees on the deck of the Cuckoo. He examines the gun in his hand, takes out the flare from the smooth nozzle and turns it around. This time, when he presses it back in, there is a click as it falls into place. A spring causes the trigger to go rigid with tension. Danny is sure it is loaded.

The boat rocks to the other side, goes down and then up a wave and rolls back. The feeling does not now make Danny feel sick. He can hear the barking of Jim deep inside the ship far below and the slow banging of Mike Heather on his cabin door. It is as if he is looking through someone else's eyes again as he moves under the wheelhouse, shielded from the windows as he is at this angle. He does not know how he will do it exactly, but he will shoot the Scotsman with the flare gun. Perhaps he will open the door, aim, and squeeze the trigger. Maybe he will wait until this Bull turns around to face him.

This is all unchartered and unknown territory for Danny, but then everything has been for this whole trip. From the moment he put on his rubber fishing gloves, everything has been a total shock, from ripping out cod livers to feeling the saltwater in his wellies. Perhaps Danny should get help from the engineer or try to get the Rat out of the fish room, maybe he should hide and hope this all passes and that the Cuckoo is swallowed by the North Sea around him.

On the horizon not a great distance away, Danny sees the lights of another boat. It will be here soon, he imagines. There is no time. He must do whatever he is going to do now.

He grips the ladder tight with one hand as he makes his way to the wheelhouse and keeps looking up to make sure the door does not swing open. It has begun to rain, and he is frozen to the bone so that he can hardly hold the flare gun in his slender hand. He bobs down when he gets to the door and then peeps up through the little window by the side. The ginger man is at the wheel and is big, much bigger than Danny thought. He has wide shoulders and a huge back; his hands are thick with freckles and strong from graft with his neck solid to his body. All Danny has to do is open the door, point the gun, and squeeze the trigger, and this will all be over. That's all he has to do. Not a thing more, and he will be warm and safe. He will get Greasy Joe to take the wheel while he finds the key to the skipper's cabin. All will be well, and in a flash, he will be back home on Woodcock Street at home in bed with his feet warm and a blanket over him. It will all be okay. His mother will be cooking him steak pie with gravy while the cat purrs on his chest. He sees the hulking shape of his father, red-faced and drunk, a belt in his hand as he beats Danny with it.

It won't be okay.

As the seconds tick down, he watches the lights from the other boat get nearer. He knows he will never get home whether he wants to or not. He will never go back to that house in that state, and he will never again let that man do what he has done to him again. His mother cannot cook steak pie well, and the cat does not like to sit on him at all. There is no need to be afraid, he realises, because the sea will have him if she wants him. Like Mike Heather says, there's nothing you can do about it.

Danny opens the wheelhouse door quickly, he levels the flare gun as he steps in and pulls the trigger. Like before, he expects a flash of light and an explosion. He expects to see the big Scotsman blown back across the little cabin. This time, the flare fizzes, and hisses. The ginger man turns to him, a washed-out lad standing at the wheelhouse door.

"It's probably out of date," he says in his thick Scottish accent. He does not look particularly shocked.

The Scotsman steps from the wheel and slaps the gun from Danny's hand like he is a child, and it clatters against the wall and splits in two. He grabs the lad by his arm, hauls him into the wheelhouse and then tosses him against the row of little windows like he is a rag doll. Danny feels a rib pop in his chest and he hits his head on the glass. He crumples to the floor and ends up crouched against the wall with his ears ringing.

"Wee bastard," says the Scott. His accent is unfamiliar and yet strangely honest. He goes back to the wheel and looks out of the window in front, then glances at Danny in the corner to make sure he's no threat. "You've got balls," he says. "I'll give you that. I told them all that we should stick to pinching boats from Grimsby. Last one I did, the crew were like wee puppies, they practically thanked me, they did, for leaving them alone. You lot, well," the Bull shakes his head. "There's only been the engineer who listens to instruction. The rest of you lot are like rabid dogs. Are you like the engineer, son? Or are you like the rest of the crew?" Danny stares up at him. He is frightened, but he has seen the look on the Scotsman's square-jawed face before; the smug sense of achievement and arrogance that comes from winning, a feeling of entitlement when the strong dominate the weak. He's seen it before on his father's face.

"I'm like the crew," replies Danny. He will not let anyone hit him anymore, whoever they are. He uses the wall to help him stand, and he feels for the fish knife in the front pocket of his dungarees under his jumper—the one with a broken handle. He does not think about what he is about to do and jumps forward at the Scotsman. The ginger man responds with a smug grin at an angry child. The Bull's mother dragged him up along the worst streets of Dundee, and the string of uncles who tortured him made violence the only currency he understands. He ignores Danny's arms and grabs him by the throat then pushes him up against the back wall.

The boy's attack is unskilled and weak, pathetic even, and the Scotsman pins his scrawny neck in his rough, freckled hands with his two big thumbs on Danny's throat.

Like he has been doing for the last week or more, Danny stabs the knife in and cuts. He goes deep through this man's jumper and stomach, sawing as he draws the knife through, letting the sharp blade do the work, just as he has done on so many codfish, right in, to get at the liver. Although the broken handle hurts his palm, he puts force into it and his knuckles go right in when he reaches the other side of the Bull's stomach. He twists the blade and withdraws. The pressure on his neck subsides as the Bull staggers back and removes his hands. The man is confused as he looks down at the wound the boy has cut in him. How could this happen? He feels terror replacing anger as blood seeps down his khaki camouflaged trousers and over his hands that go to the wound. He falls back against the broken radio. Danny has sliced open the lining of his stomach and under the bottom of his belly button, his insides are falling out. The shock of it makes the Scotsman struggle to breathe and his nostrils flare. He puts his arm over the gash to stop the blood and prevent, what he feels are his guts, from spilling out on the wheelhouse floor. He drops to his knees.

Out of the window, Danny can see the lights of the other trawler perhaps half a mile away. He grabs the wheel of the Cuckoo and brings her to the starboard side and away from the lights. His hands are shivering and there is blood on the wheel. Danny does not know whose blood it is.

CHAPTER SEVENTEEN

Danny cannot leave the wheel. The trawler banks to the starboard side. He does not want to turn her so much that she keels over, but he must get away from the lights of the other vessel. His hands shiver and his left knee knocks against the panels under the wheel. Danny has never driven a car and is not really any good with a pushbike but if he leaves this now, then they will surely be boarded. The big Scotsman kneels on the floor a few feet away and blood pools around him. Danny must think quickly. He needs the skipper.

"I want the keys to the cabins. Where are they?" he asks the Scotsman. The ginger man is beginning to go white with loss of blood and shock.

"You've killed me," he says in his Dundee accent. The trawler creaks as it banks to one side. "You've bloody killed me," he repeats. His shock gives way to anger. "You know, when those boys from the rig get on board here, they're gonna tear pieces off you one by one you can be sure of that, you wee bastard. They're not as nice as I am."

Danny continues to bank the trawler and looks down at the telegraph wheel that communicates with the engineer; he's seen the skipper move it before. He does the same. He turns it to full speed and the little bell clangs twice. It clangs twice again as Greasy Joe hears him from the engine room and he increases the engine speed. The Cuckoo complains at the strain.

"They'll slice your balls clean off," barks the Scotsman. "You'll scream. Believe me, they are men who know about that sort of thing. You'll bleed. You'll wish you weren't born. You'll cry till you're sick." Before he stops to think what he's doing, Danny picks up the long-handled spanner from the dashboard, the one the skipper uses to keep his newspaper from blowing away; turns, and smacks the Scotsman across the head with the heavy end. There's a dull thud as it cracks his skull, but he does not fall. He remains on his knees with his arm over the enormous cut in his stomach. Danny is not angry. He just has a job to do. Like any fisherman, he can't afford to mess about with too much talking when there is real work to be done.

"Keys," he repeats. A big drool of saliva gathers and falls from the Scotsman's mouth. He has been made dumb by the blow. His eyes swim.

The Rat appears at the door. The thin young man does not seem anymore scared than usual as he looks at Danny and then down at the injured Scotsman who is still reeling from the blow Danny gave him.

"I saw you in the wheelhouse," says the Rat. "They s-s-shut me in the fish room but I p-p-pushed open the hatch onto deck." Danny once more returns back to the wheel and looks out the front window. The Cuckoo is nearing the edge of its turn and will go over if Danny pushes it any harder; he begins to straighten her up.

"Go through his pockets," says Danny nodding to the injured man. The Rat looks scared. He shakes his head. There's no time for this kind of messing about. There's no time to argue. Like his mam says, if you want something doing, do it yourself. "Then grab the wheel," he commands Rat.

Danny squats down before he decides it's not a good idea. His hands go to the warm and wet blood-soaked pockets of the ginger Scotsman's camouflaged trousers. The keys are deep so he has to reach right in to get them. The stink from the man is worse than fish guts, all hot and rotten. Danny can see the little hairs that make up his ginger beard and smell the sweat from his armpits. He takes out the bunch and throws the keys up to the Rat who catches them.

"Get the crew," he says.

As the Cuckoo straightens up, the vessel behind them is still just a mass of lights. It gives chase in the silent darkness.

"At an even keel like this, we'll never outrun them," says the skipper. He has a purple swollen right cheek from where Dworkin hit him in the struggle previous, and his blue cap is tight over his head. Jim has been ordered out of the wheelhouse for sniffing and barking at the bleeding Scotsman, and the Rat is back down in the engine room with Greasy Joe. Boris inspects the injured ginger thug who has regained consciousness. He squats a good few feet away.

"Not so clever now, are you?" says the old man.

The Scott scowls back. "You're all dead men," he whispers through pale lips. Mike and Paul Heather lean against the back wall of the wheelhouse. Paul's wrists are a mess where the wire held them and Mike has a mucky angry face and a red bruise on his jaw. Sparky looks a lot better. Vicky, who is the only one who knows anything about first aid has gone to look at Dworkin out on deck. Simo has lit a cig.

"That's a good cut you've done, lad," continues Boris. It is for the Scotsman to hear. "He'll bleed out, he will. It'll take a while but he's a goner for sure. I saw a bloke got cut like that from a snapped winch cable back in the fifties. It took him ages to die. Us lads thought it would be better for him to have been washed overboard, at least it would have been quicker. He was in agony." The ginger man swallows in fear. In a fist fight he would demolish Boris, but in terms of conversation and storytelling, Boris is strong and wise; he will deliver the full weight of his powers into the Scotsman's ears. This man tried to kill Mike Heather and would probably have killed them all.

"I didn't mean to do it," says Danny.

"You did a bloody good job," says Paul Heather. "We'd none of us be standing here now if it weren't for you." It is the first time any of them have heard Paul Heather say anything nice about anyone or indeed, anything. The Scotsman has a moment of clarity.

"I told them to stay away from Hull trawlers," he says with his eyebrows raised. "I told them but that bloody Dworkin wouldn't have it."

"What were you going to do with us?" asks the skipper.

"We'll take you to Montrose, sell the fish and refit the ship. Then sell it on. We've done it before." The skipper knows the East Coast of Scotland, he knows the Scurdie Ness and the boatyard and the south of the River Esk that opens out into a vast lake. There are parts of that rugged coast where nobody ever goes. It does not surprise him, in this day and age, that they would steal a ship.

"What about the sailors? The crew? What do you do with them?" asks the skipper. The Scotsman manages a smile and there is blood on his teeth.

"Ships go down all the time in the North Sea, it's so sad. There's nobody comes looking for them." There is sarcasm on his voice. It's true. Trawlers can be lost never to be found again like the Gaul that went down the year before. Nobody knows what happened to it. The skipper's hand clenches in anger.

"Coward," whispers the skipper. "You're afraid of fishing."

"Aye, well, there's a bit more too it."

"What's the ship that's following us?"

"That's for me to know," says the Scotsman.

"Do you want us to belt you again? I can let Danny on you if you like." The skipper points across at the tall, skinny lad behind him and then down on the massive frame of the Bull. It had been David and Goliath.

"I wouldn't do that," says Boris. "We wouldn't want to put him out of his misery. He ought to feel the pain."

"You dumb trawler rats don't even know what you've got yourself into," says the Scotsman through his teeth. "It's not just about the cod. There's Russian money on the boat behind, two men from Murmansk and one from Moscow.

This is the cold war, boys. If you think I'd do this for a full fish room, you're as stupid as you are poor." He has a chuckle to himself. Like the bosun with his camera, the British government has used trawlers to spy on Russian submarines for years. It's a cheap solution and the men are going up there anyway, so why not use them to find out what the submarines are doing? Westminster knows The Soviets can fire a nuclear rocket from one of them, it's just a question of knowing where they would do it. Like Henry Boyce back in his posh office on St Andrew's Dock in Hull, better let them take the risk rather than anyone of value. Paul Heather steps forward, the ins and outs of cold war politics are not too complex for him, he just doesn't care. He feels jealousy when he looks down on the Scotsman.

"I wish I'd done that to him," he says. He has a look of genuine sadness across his face.

"Me too," says his brother with a scowl. Vicky returns to the wheelhouse. He has no smile and looks pale as well as cold.

"Dworkin's dead," he says. "You killed him, Paul." The smaller Heather boy's eyes light up and he gives the cook an honest grin.

"I did it with just my head, Mike," he says, "just my head. I had both hands behind my back." Paul holds up his bloody wrists as proof. He's proud of what he did.

"You picked the wrong boat," says the skipper to the Scotsman and the ginger man looks back up at him with frightened eyes.

"This isn't over yet, you know. There are men following. They're not trawlermen either. You've got no radio. You've got a full fish room that's slowing you down. Why not give up now, it would be easier for you?"

"Can I kill him too, skipper? I'd make it quick." Paul Heather steps forward. He makes it sound like a simple job.

"I think we should let nature take its course," he answers.

"Like Boris says, we wouldn't want to do him any favours."

"Aye," says Boris. He begins to explain to the Scotsman. "You're full of concern for us, big man, but you'll not get through this. You won't see whatever you call home or any of your family again, either." Boris's voice is full of fake worry. The Scotsman looks back at him and his lip quivers in terror.

The Scotsman is right.

The Cuckoo is not fast enough to outrun whatever is chasing her. They have a full fish room, and as the skipper straightens the wheel, his mind races. He has sent the lads back down to their bunks and kept Danny with him, for luck. They will be heavy in the water and slow to turn. They must be fifty miles off the coast. He does not know what type of craft is following them or what kind of men are on board. Russians, the Scott has told them. The skipper does not know whether to believe him or not. Boris has examined the boat approaching and they are gaining but slowly. Perhaps half an hour, he says.

It's ridiculous.

He's the skipper of a trawler, not a naval officer at war. He has to get this fish back to Hull as quickly as he can, at least before it starts to go off, that might be four days. He doesn't have time to mess about playing pirates in the North Sea. The skipper looks at the lad beside him in Sparky's radio chair. It would not be lucky to congratulate him now, this is not over. Paul Heather should not have done so, previously.

"What do you think we should do then, lad?" he asks. Any idea, even a bad one, is better than nothing.

"Shoot a flare," he says. The skipper shakes his head.

"There'll be nobody around for miles."

"We could go faster. Pull the trawl winch off and throw it in the sea."

"It's fixed to the deck."

"What about the fish, can't we dump that?" It's the reason they are all out there. The money. The green.

"We'd have to get it out by hand. It would take too long." The skipper picks his way through possibilities. They could let themselves be boarded and fight. He shakes his head. What do they already have on board? He scans the deck of the Cuckoo illuminated by the floodlights, the winch, and the baskets and then the net, rolled up and ready to be dropped on the next trip. He smiles. That's it.

"Lad," he says. "Nip down to the accommodation. I want all hands on deck. We're going fishing one last time."

The big searchlight from the vessel behind plays on the Cuckoo and the sea around. It goes from the stern and the cod liver vats to the lifeboat and the wheelhouse. Boris can see figures on the boat, silhouettes moving behind the big torch. He can hear their shouts on the wind as well. Perhaps they still believe their big, ginger-haired Scotsman is aboard. He is, but just not in the way they think. The big man is shivering, knelt on the floor of the wheelhouse with his hand across his gutted stomach and blood, now cold on his hands and legs with his face white as a freshly laundered sheet.

Skipper Bird kills the lights. He orders the ship to half speed and they turn to the port side. The men are quick to it. This is something they know and understand even in the dark. The tools are familiar in their hands. Mike Heather lifts the cod end of the trawl while Boris operates the winch. There's no need to worry about the holes in the net this time and no need to bother with the bobbins that drag it to the bottom of the ocean or the otter board. This net isn't going to the ocean floor; it's going to float on top.

Danny and Mike Heather rest the weight of it on the side of the Cuckoo, then push it over. The net slips overboard as the winch unravels slowly to let the warp cable out. The lads find hiding places on the deck.

Skipper Bird orders the engine dead slow as they turn in the darkness with their trawl net at the side of them like a slippery trap that the other vessel cannot see.

They keep the lights off.

Bring her in.

The searchlights from the boat following move over the Cuckoo in the darkness and they alter their course to pursue. The sea is not so heavy and the wind not so sharp. The skipper has had his own propellers snagged up in a trawl before, and it is a real nightmare to sort out, you just have to hope that they come unstuck on their own, somehow. There's no swimming down in the cold water to free them.

He can see the boat in more detail now as it moves closer. It's a trawler also, a different design, their trawl net goes out the stern. It's smaller as well. At the front is a man with a rope in a white oilskin outfit similar to the ones they wear on the Cuckoo. He's about the size of Simo. He holds his hand over his eyes at the boat they are moving towards so he can see. They don't look like Russians.

"Ahoy there!" he calls over the water. "Are you there, Bull? Dworkin?" It's another Scottish voice.

There is no reply from the men on board. The skipper has told them all to be as quiet as they can. Mike Heather squats behind the trawl winch with Boris. Paul Heather is not in much of a fit state for anything, but he's there behind the fish washer.

The small trawler edges forward towards the Cuckoo. It cuts off its engine and drifts and the man at the bow squints into the eerie thin fog of their searchlight. Two more figures appear.

"Dworkin!" he yells into the silent boat. "Dworkin, are you there?" There's only the slapping of the waves against the metal hulls and the creaking of cables on the masts. He throws his rope onboard the Cuckoo, it lands with a slap and he shouts again:

"Dworkin!" He listens as the nose point of his trawler drifts closer to the Cuckoo and looks up towards the wheelhouse in the darkness, to the noiseless deck. Once the bow comes close enough to the Cuckoo, he takes a step onto the side of the trawler he has been following. As he does this, Mike Heather slips from the shadows and sweeps away this man's legs with one of his powerful arms. The man slips, cracks his hip on the railings of the Cuckoo with a cry of pain before he falls between the two vessels and into the icy water below. There's a big splash and a pause before he begins to yell for help, more figures run to the bow of the smaller trawler as he shouts from below and thrashes in the freezing water. The man will be dead if his crewmates do not get him out of the sea quickly.

The skipper rings the message to Greasy Joe down in the engine room, full ahead, and the motor heart of the Cuckoo thunders into life. It's not quick, but the trawler begins to move away in the darkness amid the shouts of the other trawlermen and their mate now overboard. The searchlight from the pursuing vessels finds the wheelhouse and the open door where Skipper Bird stands in full view. He raises two fingers in glorious defiance in the glare. A shot fires in the darkness but the skipper does not duck as it ricochets off the top of the roof of the little wheelhouse.

On deck, Boris disconnects the trawl net from the winch and the warp cables. With any luck, the other trawler has already gone over it. A few feet away, Paul Heather wonders if he should make a run for it. He could leap onto the other trawler from here in one big jump. His blood is up, and anger begins in his chest. From there, he could knock them into the water like skittles, even if they are Russians, even if they have guns. He feels his fists tighten. Just as he is about to go, he feels a hand grip his collar. It's his brother, holding him back. He looks over his shoulder, and Mike shakes his head in the darkness. Just like his mam told him, Mike is there to see his older brother does not get into too much trouble.

Figures throw a life ring overboard for their mate as they shine torches into the dark sea below. He's dead if they don't get him out. The man in the water has already caught hold of the orange ring and the crew are hauling him aboard. The smaller trawler's engines fire-up and their skipper, somewhere inside their wheelhouse relays the orders to his engine room. It also bursts into action but not entirely as expected. The trawl net from the Cuckoo has engulfed them; it has gone under the bow and collected along the sides. Somewhere in the icy ocean, the ropes have got snagged around one or maybe both of the ship's propellers. It moves forward, but with nothing like the speed it should run at.

Languid and peaceful on the cold, dark sea, the Cuckoo describes a smooth arc and disappears into the thin fog of the North Water. Shots fire in the darkness and ping off the iron of the hull. There are angry shouts into the night but the little Scottish trawler with its propellers snagged, cannot go much faster than a few knots. Within a few minutes, the lights and furious yells are far away. In half an hour, it twinkles like a star on the horizon.

The Scotsman is fading very quickly in the wheelhouse. He is slumped against the wall, still on his knees. The Skipper has given him a drink of water from a tin cup but he looks pathetic. Danny's hand that cut him has not stopped shaking, and the realisation of what he has done is beginning to hit home. He believes he will face a court and a jury and prison perhaps. His life will be over. Maybe it would have been better if he hadn't been washed back on board. Like Boris always says, the sea is cruel, crueller than you can imagine.

They are all of them gathered in the wheelhouse once more. Simo smokes a cigarette. Boris jiggles his leg nervously as he leans against the wall. Vicky thinks about the soup he will make from the left-over vegetables. Paul and Mike Heather stand either side of Danny, who looks ill. The skipper is at the wheel and Sparky, who has finally come round, sits on a stool. The Rat and Greasy Joe stand close together. The apprentice engineer has swollen eyes from where he's been crying.

"I've had a few ideas, lads," says the skipper. He does not take his eyes off the darkness of the sea in front. "It will need each and every one of us to trust each other, completely." In many ways, these men already do. "We get this bastard off the floor here and we throw him overboard. Then we get Dworkin and throw him overboard too. There's no record of either of them on the books. Like the lad, the company don't know that Dworkin was ever here, that Scott neither." The skipper begins. "We get the bosun out of the fish room and dump him as well. We say he got washed overboard when we get nearer home." For the first time, the skipper turns to look at his crew. "There's no point in going through all the crap that we'd have to go through, the investigation or the explanations." He turns back to the sea. "The bosun was an arsehole anyway. We all thought that. Even Jim." The men do not make any sound behind him. He must continue to sell them the idea. "This way Boris, you can get on with moving to Hornsea. You'll be in Rayners on Thursday or Friday night, Paul, with a pint in your paw. You'll get to see the misses, Sparky. Lad here can see his mam, so can you, Simo. Joe, you can see your mates. Vicky, you can get applying for college or whatever. We all get to put a full stop after all this. We can just forget it ever happened."

Danny lets out a sigh, he cannot contain it. It's fear.

"I don't wanna go to jail," he says. "I didn't mean to kill him." The skipper turns on his heel and his voice is hot with anger.

"You, lad, have got nothing to cry about, you're a bloody hero. Every one of us here owes you for what you did. Do you understand? We defended ourselves like anyone would. That's all." The skipper points to the dying man in the corner of the wheelhouse. "I would have done the same. He would have done worse to you. If they were Russians on that ship following us, they would have dumped us all at the bottom of the sea, all of us, without another thought." The skipper regains his composure and turns back to the water and the night in front. The radar blips below him, the little motor on the storm window hums, the Cuckoo rides the waves below.

"So, after this conversation is over," he continues, "there's a new truth about what happened here. Do you all understand? You never met Dworkin and you never knew a man by that name. You never saw a big ginger Scotsman. Sparky hit his head in a swell. Paul got into a fight with his brother, Mike, which explains their faces and mine and Joe's for breaking it up. We caught fish. We sailed back to Hull. That's it. That's what happened. As we came past Withernsea, the bosun was out on deck taking photos with his camera, and he got washed overboard." The noise from the engine below purrs. The rain begins against the windows. The trawler creaks with the weight of the catch in the fish room.

"Aye," says Paul Heather. He still has blood and bits of Dworkin down the front of his coat.

"Yup," says Simo. He crushes his cig out below his boot. Sparky rubs the side of his head where he was whacked and then nods.

"Me and the Rat will go along with it," says Greasy Joe.

"Aye," says Mike Heather. Vicky nods. He will get his head kicked in if he doesn't agree.

"I hated that bosun," says Boris, "but he didn't deserve to get washed overboard not after all them years at sea. His poor misses. You would have radioed straight away, skipper, if Sparky here hadn't hit his head on the VHF radio."

"She'll be over the moon," says Paul Heather without

emotion.

"Just you then, lad," says the skipper. "What do you say?" Danny looks around him at the faces. The wrinkles on old Boris, the cruel eyes of Paul Heather glaring, Sparky with his blonde, brill-creamed hair.

"So, what did happen to the bosun?" asks Danny. "The Scotsman wouldn't have hit him, it was before we got started fishing." Paul Heather frowns.

"Maybe he did hit his head," says the skipper.

"Maybe you did it to him," says Paul Heather. The skipper's cool eyes regard the men.

"What does it matter?" says Boris. "He's gone and it's not the worst thing."

"What do you say, lad?" asks the skipper. Danny looks down at the steel floor and his hands go to his forehead. He's been through a lot.

"Aye, that's what happened," he whispers.

"That's it done then," says the skipper.

Mike and Paul Heather carry the cold body of the Scotsman down the steps of the wheelhouse and toss it overboard without ceremony. They find Dworkin laid on his back on the deck, carry him by his hands and feet and swing him into the darkness, then hear the splash as he hits the water. Boris goes to the lifeboat, he shakes his head when he finds the fur-lined sleeping bag, the empty bottle of scotch and tins of salmon, the chocolate wrappers and a torch. There's a bottle of milk from Vicky's kitchen.

"He's been all over the boat," he mutters to himself. Boris chucks the whole lot into the sea as well.

Down in the bosun's room, the skipper opens the drawers in his desk and pulls out the expensive camera in its leather case. He takes out the long lenses and the ring-bound books full of illustrations of Russian boats. There's his notebook too with the numbers of all the vessels he's seen in tiny writing under the dates. The skipper wonders how much he got for this? The bosun won't have been cheap.

In the fish room, three of them, Paul, Mike, and Danny remove the first wooden slat they put there and slide out the body of the bosun. He looks thin, and his skin is drawn back to his cheekbones, his knees are bent to his chest. They carry his frozen body up onto deck where the skipper is waiting and lay it down on a piece of netting in front of the trawl winch. All the crew are there apart from Greasy Joe in the wheelhouse.

Boris considers saying something mystical, like 'there'll be a price to pay', but he doesn't think any of them killed this tall, serious man. It's not their fault he is cold and dead on the deck, even if they didn't like him and he did have it coming. The skipper clutches his cap in both hands. Sparky has a cig on the go and his collars up. It's freezing in the darkness. Danny's face is without expression. Boris ties both ends of the net around the man and attaches two spare bobbins so the body will fall to the bottom of the North Sea. The skipper does not think it wise for the bosun to wash ashore, and for people to see the wound on the side of his head. He's not bothered about Dworkin or The Bull, they never knew those men anyway and there is no connection to them. Mike and Danny lift the body onto the side of the Cuckoo, and it rests there for a few moments.

"Goodbye, bosun," says the skipper. "Rest in peace." They let the body roll off and it splashes into the seawater below. The skipper throws his camera and the books after him, and they all bow their heads; each man is alone with his thoughts for a minute.

Danny imagines the bosun's body falling through the icy waters backwards, pulled down and down by the bobbins in the darkness.

He sees it in his dreams for many years to come.

CHAPTER EIGHTEEN

At St Andrew's Dock, the tugboat pilot has a fat gut with a white shirt under his dungarees. He's not dressed for being outside and he shouts up at the skipper from beside his own wheelhouse on the deck of his little but powerful boat. The skipper stands at the stern of the Cuckoo and explains. This pilot is angry and having a lot off, because the radio is broken and they haven't been able to call ahead, he didn't know the Cuckoo was due in. It has screwed up his lunchtime.

Danny stands on the deck and looks up at the imposing building and the words 'Lord Line' embossed in stone on the front. It feels like more than ten years since he was last here. It's a Thursday afternoon, the day that Paul Heather believes is the best day to return.

At Kilnsea, the Cuckoo was spotted by the coast guard, and they would have radioed back to the office the ship was in one piece and was on its way home, they should have told the tug. The gates of the big dock open and the tugboat pushes the Cuckoo through. The skipper guides the trawler into place against the dock, and Mike Heather throws the big ropes to the lads who tie the vessel on cleats.

The dock is alive with business. Along the quayside, two other ships are being unloaded. A crane swings a basket onto the deck of one that drops into the fish room, Below Men inside will fill it before it gets winched up. It's a whole industry in itself getting the fish out, there are scrubbers who will clean the boards, barrow lads, winch men and those who weigh the fish. That's even before it gets sold. Paul Heather watches the workers line up ready to unload the fish from the Cuckoo. He's done his job, he'll let them do theirs.

The ship's husband and runner, Tadman, steps up the gangplank and onto the Cuckoo. He has a ginger beard, and a woolly cap pulled down to just above his eyes. The skipper meets him at the door to the wheelhouse. Here's the man who didn't fill them up with enough diesel or find enough crew. The Cuckoo is Tadman's trawler now. He inspects the broken radio with a dent in the front.

"How the bloody hell did this happen?"

"Sparky's head," answers the skipper. The floor has been scrubbed like the whole ship. Tadman looks at Richard Bird with a scowl over his long, pointed nose.

"I don't believe you," he says in his parroty voice.

"Sparky fell over in a swell and hit it." answers the skipper. Tadman scowls.

"How much have you got?" He means fish. Now they are not at sea the skipper can say without sounding boastful.

"Two hundred tonne, I reckon." Tadman is both happy and unhappy about this. He had wanted Skipper Bird to fail and come back with nothing so that he would lose his ticket and have to wear out a pair of boots walking to find another job. But a big haul means more money for everyone. This is good. "We lost one of the trawl nets, we had to cut it off, it got snagged on the seafloor."

"It'll come out your wages," snaps Tadman, "like this bloody radio will. We thought you'd gone down, you know, like the Gaul. We thought you'd been lost." Skipper Bird smiles.

"You wish," he says.

"I don't give a toss about you, Birdie, either way, but I care about this ship and about the fish in the hold."

"There's another thing," says the skipper. It's best to get bad jobs over with as quickly as you can. "It happened on the way back when we hit rough seas. I don't know how or what he thought he was doing." The skipper's mouth is suddenly dry. "It was the bosun, Oliver Jackson, he went overboard. He was taking pictures with that big camera he has, we were just off Withernsea."

Tadman takes off his cap and runs his hands over his bald

head in thought. He frowns at the skipper. It's not a good thing for another trawlerman to die, they have enough bad press as it is. He tuts, partly because it's not nice to hear about a man losing his life, but also because Oliver Jackson, the dead bosun, had promised him a backhander if he got him the skipper's ticket when Birdie here screwed it up.

"You'll have to tell his misses," snaps Tadman. "It's your bloody fault. I wish I could take that out of your wages as well."

"I'm off to tell her now," says the Skipper. "I haven't had to do it before." It's not a thing he has been looking forward to.

"Do you want me to give you some advice?" Tadman's tone is sarcastic and yet humorous. You never know where you are with him or if he's on your side.

"I think I'll be alright."

"You think you'll be alright," mocks Tadman. He was a skipper himself, he's done it before. "There'll be screaming and crying and that's if you're lucky. I've had wives try to tear my eyes out before now, cups thrown at me, sons and uncles threaten to beat me up, even dogs try to attack me." Tadman enjoys inflicting this cruelty.

"What do you care about any of that?" asks the skipper. "I've brought you back all the fish you need. You didn't fill us up with enough fuel and where were my extra crew?" The runner swipes away the questions with a flick of his hand in the air, as if they aren't important. He gives a huff and inspects the gyroscope, the gauges, and the smashed radio.

"It's easy for you lot," he says. "You young uns don't know what it's like. I sailed a steam trawler for thirty-five years. We had no electricity, no heating, no bloody radio. You kids have got all the creature comforts these days." Tadman notices the crack in the windowpane on the wheelhouse, where somebody might have smashed the bosun's head or maybe where the Scotsman threw Danny.

"That'll come out of your wages as well," he says. The skipper hopes he does not notice the bullet dint above the door.

On the deck, standing at the gangplank, the skipper waits for his crew. He is going to get off last. This is what he always does when they get home. Mike Heather clumps up from the accommodation with his kitbag over his shoulder. There's no need for ceremony now, and no need to worry about superstitions or things that are green. The job is done. The fish are caught. He shakes the skipper's hand and then walks across the plank. Paul comes next. He gives a limp shake. Then Vicky with a grin. Simo approaches.

"That was a good one," he says. Ever sarcastic. Greasy Joe and the Rat follow with handshakes and their eyes down. Then Boris. Finally, there's young Danny. He looks better than he did a few days earlier but there's still a sadness to him. The skipper claps him on the back and follows him up onto the concrete of dry land. The crew from the Cuckoo stand together and an old woman with a headscarf breaks through the bobbers, who are already climbing about the ship to unload the fish. The woman's face is at once weeping and full of joy as she goes towards Boris with open arms.

"Oh Arthur," she cries out, "when we hadn't heard from you, we thought you'd been lost. Like the Gaul, we thought you'd gone down. You always did say you'd get lost at sea." Boris is really called Arthur. Arthur Lewandowski. He throws his arms around the woman who is his wife.

"I thought we were going over at one point, LeeAnn." He smiles at her after he has kissed her on the lips.

"That's it now then, love, you're finished with the sea," she says. Boris nods:

"I'm done." She beams back and they embrace.

"And you didn't die at sea, in the end, even though that horrible woman from Liverpool Street read it in your mum's tea leaves." Arthur 'Boris' Lewandowski will live well into his early nineties and will die at home in bed survived by his daughter, who becomes a biology lecturer up at the university. He will feel guilty that many friends disappeared into the ocean and he did not. The two of them walk off past the bobbers arm in arm and down towards the bustle and life of Hessle Road.

The rest of the crew move on, and taxis wait in a line away from the noise and shouts of the working dock. They know that fisherman just back from sea will be loaded, and they will sometimes use the same cab for the full three days they are home. Simo and Paul get into the first one without saying good-bye, the engine starts and they are gone.

Paul will go to sea for the next few years even after St Andrew's Dock closes in November 1975, and even after the Cod Wars take their final toll and fishing is limited to beyond a two-hundred-mile radius off Iceland. Then he will go to the factories. After the killing of Dworkin with just his head and mouth, Paul has a much more relaxed attitude. Although he never tells another soul about it, he is glad. It proves he is worthy of being his father's fighting son.

Simo works another season on the boats before picking up his bass again. His original band, The Kestrels, reform when the singer gets out of jail and he makes a go of it on the road where he's happy.

The Rat and Greasy Joe don't get a taxi. Joe will go looking for girls at one of the places he knows, and the Rat will walk home to his house on Witty Street where his mam will cook him a roast chicken dinner. He won't say a word about the trip and they will never ask.

Vicky is not flash enough to get a taxi and would rather walk than spend his money. He does make it to the big college in the town centre in the end, after a couple more seasons on the trawlers, and eventually buys a greasy spoon van which he parks on a slip road off the A1079 to York.

The skipper wants to walk on dry land rather than ride in anything, even though it's cold. He fits a thin rope lead to Jim's collar. He and the dog have one more job to do.

"Come on then, Bill," he says to the little dog.

"I thought he was called Jim," says Danny.

"He is on the boat, lad," says the skipper. He walks a few paces leaving Mike and Danny waiting but then turns as if he's forgotten something.

"What's your name again?" he asks.

"Danny. Danny Green," the skipper purses his lips at the second name.

"It was good to sail with you, Danny. You're the finest deckie learner I've ever come across, and I've seen more than a few." They shake hands like friends. It makes Danny feel good, like he is a real person. The lad reaches into the inside pocket of his donkey jacket and pulls out the yellow envelope, the caul that the skipper gave him for protection.

"This is yours," he says as he holds it out. The skipper smiles and shakes his head.

"Keep it, Danny Green, on me."

He and Mike Heather watch the skipper and Jim cross over the road into West Dock Ave, the two of them blend into the bustle of the street.

Mike goes to the door of another taxi and holds it open. Danny looks at him with a quizzical face.

"I'm giving you a lift home," says the big man.

The dog and Skipper Richard Bird walk side by side like good friends down Hessle Road. At the top of Gillett Street, they turn. The sky is dark. It looks like it might rain or even snow with this cold. He walks all the way down to number 66 and taps on the front door, conscious for the first time he is the bad news every fisherman's wife and family have seen in their nightmares.

The door opens and an old woman looks out at him with

a creased, miserable face and a scowl. The skipper can see this is the bosun's mam from the demeanour.

"Can I come in please, Mrs Jackson?" he asks. She does not say anything as she beckons him through into the front room. There, sat on the arm of the sofa is the bosun's thin wife. She has a bruise on her cheek that she has covered with makeup. They will already have been told he hopes. News can travel quickly between the people of Hessle Road where everyone knows everyone else. In fact, just the skipper's presence at the house is evidence her husband is not coming back. He takes off his hat and holds it in his hands like he always does.

"Get on with it then," says the bosun's mam.

"We were 16 miles north of Withernsea or thereabouts. Rough weather. He was taking his pictures with that camera he loved so much. He was there one minute and then not the next. We looked for him but the waves were just too bad, after a few minutes he would have been gone anyway. I'm sorry, Mrs Jackson, and Mrs Jackson." The thin woman puts her hand to her face and the older one wears no expression at all as she nods.

"Thank you for coming straight away," she says. The dog looks up at her through his brown eyes and the thin wife with the bruise considers the man, standing in her front room.

"I am, truly sorry for your loss," he says. It's genuine.

"Do you know what it's like to lose something you love, skipper?" she asks. He thinks about his wife back at home and the baby that should be already in the box bedroom he decorated, sleeping in the white cot he built.

"Aye, I do," he says. The skipper takes a deep breath.

"I'll see you out," says the bosun's mam.

The thin wife breaks down when he has gone, her face is in both hands as she weeps over the expensive rug.

They are tears of joy.

Danny has never been in a taxi. It feels strange to be on the comfy seats in the back with Mike Heather next to him, watching the busy folk of Hessle Road out of the windows as they drive to Woodcock street. It is not a long journey, and so it's very decadent to get a taxi for such a short distance, but their catch has been huge. With so few of them on board, the money they will pick up the next day from the office will be substantial. After the bobbers have unloaded it and then fish traders have sold it, the tally will be big. Especially since it will get sold as fresh on the biggest day of the week for selling fish, Friday. The deckie learner will get more than the fifty quid the skipper promised him.

Danny tells the driver where he lives and the black cab stops outside his little terraced house. He gets out. There's nothing different about Woodcock Street, not the telephone wires that connect the houses above, or the grey sky or his neighbour's scrubbed front step, or the net curtains in his front window so no one can see in. His mouth is dry and his hands are shaking. He does not want to be here and he does not want to face the anger of his father. Danny might rather face the North Sea again instead.

"Where to now, boss?" says the taxi driver to Mike.

"Just wait," says the big man. He has wound down the window so he can speak to the lad. His breath makes mist in the cold, late Thursday afternoon air. "Danny, if you need me, I'll be here, mate." Mike has a very long memory, a keen sense of right and wrong and an empathy that his brother has never understood. He will not ever forget what this tall and skinny lad has done for him.

Danny takes a deep breath and walks down the alley at the side to the back yard. This is the way anyone who is not important enters the house. His palms are sticky as he pushes opens the gate, his palms clammy, and a light film of sweat gathers across his brow. Every instinct he has tells him to run, but he knows he has to face the old man. Where will he go otherwise?

Danny stands nervously at the back door, then opens it and steps through into the kitchen. His father will have just woken up after having been on the nightshift, he is dressed in his pyjamas. Danny's mam drops her knife when she sees him. Her husband stands and his eyes are wide and still misty from whatever he drank the night before:

"Where the bloody hell have you been?" He is instantly red hot with anger, his hands go into fists. Danny is ready for him. He has taken the advice of someone who knows what to do in such situations. At the end of his lanky arm, Danny closes his own fist into Mike Heather's clothesline. It is what he will deliver to the back of his father's head, and he will tell the man never to strike him or his mam ever again, nor to raise his voice against them either. It will be the change they need.

Time stops for a second.

As soon as his father begins his movement, Danny plans to step to the right and swing the clothesline to the back of his head. He can see his father's teeth are tight together under a snarl. Just as he is about to attack his son, there are two urgent thumps at the front door.

They stop.

Danny's mam passes between the two and goes to the living room and the front door. They follow. It wouldn't be right to have a domestic with someone listening. What would people think? She opens the door and there, dressed in his mucky seafaring clothes, is Mike Heather. He has his beanie hat in his hands as a show of manners.

"Can I come in?" he asks. The taxi waits just behind him with the engine ticking over. "I'm a friend of Danny's." The woman nods and steps back to let him in. In the front room, which is ordinarily only for important people, Mike Heather is out of place. He is used to noisy pubs and unsteady fish decks and dwarfs Danny's father as he stands, looking nervously at the little family. Mike is out of his comfort zone, he knows how to gut fish and drink and sometimes fight, he does not know how to talk. He remembers that Danny faced off the big Scotsman who had bested him. He has to try.

"It doesn't have to be like this," says Mike. He knows the way this works. Danny attacks his father, whether he wins or loses, the outcome will be exactly the same and the circle of violence will continue, just as it did in his house. "You don't have to hit him, Danny. It shouldn't be like that." Tears form in Mike's big eyes. "I ended up belting the hell out of my father, and it didn't do us any good, neither of us."

"What do you want?" snaps Danny's father. He pretends not to know what Mike is talking about, but this fisherman has a straightforward way of telling the truth, not to be cruel or kind, but to be honest.

"I want to tell you what a good lad your boy is. How well he did. How he helped all of us and how you should be bloody proud of him just the way he is." The truth is not always bad. Sometimes it is just obvious. Danny really is a good, strong lad. Mike rubs his face with his hand. It has taken a lot out of the big man to say this. A tear runs down the side of his face though he does not show any other emotion. This is what he wished someone had said to his father; for that is all he really wanted from the man, for him to be proud of his son. "He's been away at sea," Mike continues. "He got washed overboard and back on again and…" the big man struggles at words that will not form, his chest has tightened and he takes a breath: "he's my bloody mate."

Mike has done well.

Nobody could have heard the words and failed to understand. Danny's father nods in gratitude.

After this, it's like the floodgates have opened. His mam sobs as she hugs her son. Even though he still stinks of fish, he is home. When she is done, Danny's father claps him on the shoulder as he has never done before and, although they will argue in the days and years to come, it will never again be as it was. There is a steel to Danny his father must now contend with, and mettle that the old man must admire. Mike nods his thanks and backs out the door.

In the taxi home, the big man cries silently and behind his hands. The driver pretends not to notice. The tears are not for what has happened with Danny or the bosun or the fight with the Scot, but for his own father and the relationship that he never had with the man. Mike will rise to be a mate, then bosun, then skipper and will emigrate to South Africa when the bottom falls out of the trawler business completely. He will grow to be a big, warm man like his mother wanted him to become. He is the last of generations of brave, hard men who brought fish back in through St Andrew's Dock since it opened in 1883.

It takes the skipper and Bill twenty minutes to walk all the way down Boulevard and past the church. The street is lined with trees on either side. On a summer day it's green and pretty, but today under a grey sky the oaks are bare. The solid ground makes the skipper feel strange after so many weeks at sea, and the noise of the street and the cars are foreign to his ears. Though he has travelled all over the North Water, the skipper is always at home when he is on the Cuckoo.

Not anymore.

He stops outside a yellow brick terrace with a tiny front garden and looks it up and down.

He is home.

Standing in front of the door before he opens it, he looks down at Bill. This is it. He's made his promise. If he walks in, his life will change forever. For a second the skipper checks over his shoulders back down The Boulevard and towards St Andrew's Dock, the River Humber and the Great North Sea. He feels the sting of longing and already, he misses standing in that wheelhouse and the smell of the salt spray, the worry of where they will catch and the joy of watching a full trawl spill out on the fish deck.

The door is not locked. Inside the skipper sets down his kit bag and slips off his shoes. He lets Bill off his lead, but the little dog remains by his side. In the kitchen down the corridor, she sits at the table with her hand around a mug of tea. She looks washed out but beams as her husband enters. He takes off his blue skipper's cap and his eyes fill with tears as she touches the smooth bump of her stomach, their first. The skipper loves the ocean under his feet, he loves the open horizon of the sea, to be a hunter with his lads, ready to face everything the North Sea has to the throw at them.

He loves all this, but he loves her more.

"Your father's home," she says.

#

Printed in Germany
by Amazon Distribution
GmbH, Leipzig